REUNION WITH MURDER

by

Oswald G. Ragatz

This book is a work of fiction. Places, events, and situations in this story are purely fictional. Any resemblance to actual persons, living or dead, is coincidental.

© 2001 by Oswald G. Ragatz. All rights reserved.

No part of this book may be reproduced, stored in a retrieval system, or transmitted by any means, electronic, mechanical, photocopying, recording, or otherwise, without written permission from the author.

ISBN: 0-7596-4165-X

This book is printed on acid free paper.

1stBooks - rev. 10/19/01

Note to the Reader

The author is a native of Colorado, but except for brief, occasional visits, he has not been in the State for five decades. References to specific Colorado problems are based solely on mention in national periodicals and on comments of friends who still live in that glorious State.

CHAPTER 1

During our twenty-three years of marriage, my wife Lucille had never displayed any signs of jealousy. I was never sure whether she had implicit trust in my fidelity or whether she figured I didn't have enough initiative to embark on any extramarital affairs. There were even times when I thought maybe she didn't care whether I was faithful to her or not. One can never tell about wives—or oneself, for that matter. I'd not given her any cause to be jealous. A few minor flirtations had been carried out with the utmost discretion, and indeed I had not brought any of these to any sort of fruition, whether because of moral rectitude or for lack of gumption (an archaic word probably belonging to an earlier generation). I couldn't tell without the help of a good shrink.

At any rate, because of her past record, my wife's tone of voice and the quizzical look on her face was quite startling as she relayed the message to me. I'd just gotten home from a late afternoon faculty committee meeting of the Political Science Department of DeMott University, that private Midwestern institution of higher learning which had only recently found it possible to recognize my twenty years of service as its senior professor of Political Science by promoting me to a full professorship. Lucille greeted my peck on her mouth with more than her usual detachment, indicating that something was amiss. So I waited as she continued stirring something in a pot on the stove. I knew that shortly I would be facing the necessity of making some sort of rejoinder, I assumed for some oversight or infraction of domestic protocol. That type of thing I usually take in stride, and I might say that I am pretty adept at holding my own in the domestic arena. But I wasn't prepared for what was to ensue.

Oswald G. Ragatz

With a glint in her eye—or was it a twinkle—but with a definite edge to her voice, Lucille said, "Marilou called you from Colorado."

Now I supposed that some time in the past I might have mentioned to Lucille the existence of Marilou Baxter, one time college girlfriend, but I wasn't sure. I'd not thought of Marilou for years. I think I once read in a psych. book that in the long run we tend to remember the pleasant events of our past but forget—block out—the unpleasant. And memories of Marilou were certainly unpleasant. Well, not all of them, *au contraire*! But the events that led to the termination of our relationship were most unpleasant indeed.

I'm sure that a number of expressions flitted across my mobile features. I say my features are mobile because Lucille tells me I can't hide a thing; "Just look at your face!" she'll say. But by the time I get to the mirror on those few occasions when I take her advice, all I see is the usual dead pan I shave every morning, and the same set of teeth I brush twice a day, and the receding hairline backed by slightly fuzzy graying hair. So that my face was mobile now I had no doubt. Lucille was looking at me intently, with slightly lowered eyelids, and I suddenly knew I was going to blush. I didn't know what I'd do if I ever really had something to feel guilty about.

Obviously I was supposed to say something, so I tried my best to sound nonchalant and slightly disinterested.

"Well, I'll be damned. I'd forgotten all about her. What did she want, for Pete's sake?"

I took an apple from a bowl on the counter, though I don't really like apples, and bit into it, partly to hide a small part of my face and partly to keep me from gaping at Lucille.

For a few moments I thought Lucille had forgotten all about it. She concentrated on whatever it was in the pot on the stove, then reaching for a pot holder, she removed the pan and set it over on the sink counter.

"Supper will be ready in a few minutes. We're having this soup for a first course. I saw the recipe in The Family Circle."

Then, just when I thought I must have imagined that Lucille had mentioned Marilou, she added, "Marilou says that she SOOO much hopes you will be coming to the class reunion, and that she and all the old gang will be SOOO looking forward to seeing you again after all these years."

Well, no rejoinder came to mind, and I forgot to put the apple to my gaping mouth, which gave Lucille the chance to administer the *coup de grace*, in the sweetest, most reasonable tone of voice you can imagine, but I wasn't fooled, not for a minute.

"I really think you should go. It's the second week in June, and that's when Mother is breaking up the house and moving into her new apartment, so I can go to Columbus to help her, and you can go out and give THE OLD GANG a treat, and Marilou, of course."

I hasten to add that the last three words were not delivered in the same reasonable tone of voice as the rest of the statement. Whatever Marilou had said, or more likely how she said it, certainly had gotten under Lucille's skin. I could tell.

I'd received some publicity about the twenty-fifth reunion of our class, but I had not seriously considered going all the way out to Colorado just to have old memories dredged up. Don't get me wrong. Much of my college undergraduate experience had been fun. But the senior year was pure hell and heartbreak. The disillusionment following the termination of one's first love is frequently traumatic. The prospect of encountering old ghosts did not interest me in the least. Any thought I might have had of going to the reunion had been dismissed when I read that the speaker at the final banquet would be Senator Robert Henry Wexler. If there was anyone I didn't want to see again, let alone listen to at a banquet, it was Bob Wexler. When I said I'd not thought of Marilou for years that wasn't quite true. Everytime I'd seen Senator Wexler's name mentioned in the press during the past four years, I perforce had thought of Marilou. Not that Bob Wexler was one of the country's leading legislators. Quite the contrary.

But I'd not thought about Marilou's being at the reunion, and I found myself beginning to be rather intrigued with the potential of The Old Gang's being together again after twenty-five years. My Political Scientist's detachment in the act of observing the human condition was coming to the fore. If I could just maintain that detachment, it actually might be fun.

Of course, all The Old Gang would not be there. Jake Harrell had been killed during my first year in graduate school at Yale, some sort of skiing accident in the Colorado mountains. But I was beginning to consider the potential of having several of Bob Wexler's old loves "together again." Then I wondered who his present wife was, and if she would be there. I knew he and Amanda had divorced a few years after they'd been married.

Well, it was clear that MY wife wouldn't be there, and I didn't blame her a bit. I had gone with her to her twenty-fifth high school reunion two years back, and it was strictly dullsville. I'm not your basic outgoing extrovert, and being faced with several hundred strangers, all of whom seemed to know each other intimately, was a real drag. Furthermore, I had the feeling that there were times when my presence had been definitely inhibiting for Lucille. So I'd made up my mind then and there that I'd never subject my wife to the same torture. That, plus the reasons mentioned above, had made me decide not to go to my college twenty-fifth. But now my second thoughts decreed that I had better not wait for the fiftieth reunion if I ever wanted to see my old classmates again.

Nothing more was said about the reunion during dinner, but later in the evening I went to my desk in the study and found the announcement of the reunion buried under some ungraded term papers and a couple of catalogues for power tools. The committee was going all-out, with events covering most of two days and culminating in the banquet where Senator Bob Wexler would undoubtedly strut his stuff. I found Marilou's name listed with the contact committee, which explained why she had called me—or did it? Anyway, since I'm apt to follow Lucille's suggestions, I found myself filling out the form saying I'd attend.

Then I tackled the request for biographical information which turned out to be a rather rewarding task. During the last ten years there had been a number of events I now enjoyed setting down for my former classmates to read. There were three published books of considerable importance in my field, a dozen or more papers in prestigious journals, and a guest lectureship during a summer term at my graduate alma mater, Yale. Then there was Lucille, Associate Professor in Fine Arts, and two children embarking on their various careers with (we hoped) promise. I was tempted to mention that the mortgage on the house would be paid up in another two years, but decided that, along with such things as thinning hair and increased waist line, that bit of information could be omitted.

As I ran my eyes down the publicity brochure again, I saw that the contact committee members had listed their phone numbers. On an impulse, and hearing the television roaring away in the living room where Lucille sat knitting, I dialed Marilou Baxter's number. It was a Colorado area code. As the phone was ringing, I had just time to realize that she still used her maiden name, so possibly she had never married. But of course, one can't be sure these days, what with divorces, women's lib, and all.

I almost panicked, but Marilou answered before I had a chance to hang up. Indeed, when she said "Hello, this is Marilou Baxter" in that almost babyish but seductive voice, I knew I should have hung up. There was a stab of something that resembled pain right through the solar plexus. In an instant time warp experience, all the emotions of love and hate and disillusionment of that last year in college came back from wherever they had been lurking during all those years since. I was totally aghast at my reaction, certainly more surprised than pleased. But now there was nothing to do but to bull it through.

As it turned out, the conversation was quite reasonable. We both were detached and cool. I did ask Marilou what she had been doing the past few years—I hesitated to say the past twenty-four years—and so I found out that she was working as a librarian at our Alma Mater. The facade of detached disinterest was momentarily broken only once when she added, "I never married, you know. After Bob Wexler broke off with me, I decided I'd had enough of that sort of romance for a life time."

What she didn't have to add was that I'd refused to resume our relationship after she and Bob broke up. Shortly after Jake was killed in the skiing accident, Bob took up with Amanda Forsythe, Jake's fiance. Marilou was left out in the cold, so she took a job in Boston, giving her an excuse to hightail it to New Haven where I was in my second year of graduate school.

Well, that was an amazing twenty-four hours, and I have always been proud of myself. I wasn't having any of it, not after the way Marilou had dumped me for Bob Wexler. I took her around the campus, fed her at some good restaurants, bade her a cool good night at her hotel, and then the next morning shook hands at the bus station, sending her off to Boston. I'd been very big about it all when she broke up with me—a lot of platitudes such as whatever makes you happy makes me happy, etc. But that was it. No more. What had happened once could happen again, and I wasn't setting myself for another traumatic episode. And I'd never regretted that stand I took in New Haven, not for a second.

Marilou's mentioning Bob Wexler seemed to call for some rejoinder, so I said something to the effect that it was probably all for the good, that being married to a big-time politician would not have been an easy life.

Marilou's reply to that was a shocker.

"Well, you can say that again. He walked out on Amanda after they'd been married less than five years, and his second wife committed suicide shortly after he went to Washington. He's married now to a VonBronigan. He may see that she stays around awhile since he finally has someone with the financial resources he wants."

This was said in a voice I hardly recognized. All baby sweetness was replaced by pure vitriol. It prompted me to ask a question.

"Why is Bob being starred as lecturer for the banquet?" Marilou's voice changed to puzzlement.

"You know, I can't figure that one out. Actually, this whole reunion has been pretty much engineered by Amanda, and believe it or not it was her idea to have Bob for the banquet speaker. I was floored when she suggested featuring her ex-husband. I almost think she has some plan up her sleeve to somehow spike his campaign for reelection to the Senate, maybe a sort of revenge for the way he treated her. But I haven't been able to figure out what it could be. Well, I'm glad you're going to be here to see the fireworks, if there are any. I'm sure you have no great affection for Bob Wexler."

That was the truth! And that was the only reference to the events of our senior year. A few more pleasantries, and the conversation was ended, leaving me with quite a lot of things to think about, not that I had much time to think about them during the next six weeks. The semester was winding down, with term papers and exams to grade, final lectures to prepare, the reading and proofing of a couple of dissertations I was supervising, plus the usual plethora of committee meetings and Commencement festivities to attend.

There was a week between Commencement and my going to Colorado, so Lucille and I went to New York for a pleasant interlude which included a couple of plays, a concert, and a night or two on the town. Then it was time to leave for Denver, and I shortly found myself with several hours just to think, and the more I thought the more confused and depressed I became.

On the brief flight from Jeffreysville to Cincinnati, I only thought about the hassle of getting Lucille off to her mother's in Columbus and me packed and on the plane. But from Cincinnati to Denver my mind settled into a groove, mulling over unpleasant memories mostly.

The Old Gang had coalesced some time early in our sophomore year. As I thought about it, I realized that the term gang hardly applied. The nucleus consisted of Marilou and me and Amanda and Jake. Bob Wexler was the fifth, but he did not settle on any one girl for double or triple dating, picnics, and the like. It was a little strange as he was a very personable guy, outgoing and almost glib and could be a lot of fun to be with. He had no trouble getting dates. But he always seemed to be waiting for someone to come along and sweep him off his feet, all the while looking on at the rest of us. There were others who had floated in and out of our friendship, but the five of us constituted what Marilou had now referred to as "The Old Gang." Maybe the gang was limited to five or six by the fact that we had only one set of wheels at our disposal. Amanda's father was a senior partner in a big law firm in Denver and could afford to give her a Buick sedan to take to college. Marilou's father was a lawyer also, but the Baxters weren't in the chips like Amanda's family was.

Neither Bob nor I had any money in our backgrounds, and Jake came from a ranching family in southern Colorado. He was doing a major in business so that on graduation he could return to the ranch and run it in a business-like manner. He and Amanda were going to get married shortly after graduation, but neither Bob nor I would be ready to settle down upon receipt of the A.B. degree. I was looking forward to years of graduate study, and Bob was going to law school. Typically of the young, however, I didn't see this insecurity of the future as any deterrent to pursuing a heavy romance with Marilou. We weren't exactly engaged, as Amanda and Jake were, but we might as well have been. If it had been a decade or two later, we no doubt would have pooled our meager resources and set up housekeeping in some apartment near campus. But the social mores weren't ready for that quite yet. Nor was I ready for that sort of thing. As a matter of fact, Marilou and I had never, as we said in those days, "gone all the way."

Then this rather vacuous but lovely existence came to an abrupt termination at the fall, all-college harvest dance. Bob and his date, whose name I can't even remember, double dated with Marilou and me. (Bob had borrowed his folks car for the weekend.) It was much the custom to trade dances, and so early in the evening I found myself with Bob's date. When that dance concluded, however, Bob and Marilou were nowhere to be seen, so Bob's date and I continued to be together for another hour or so. I was embarrassed for Bob's date, but I didn't think much about it as far as Marilou was concerned, naive and besotted with love as I was. However, the rest of the evening was charged with an undercurrent of something which I didn't understand.

The situation began to clarify, alas, during the next week. Marilou told me she was going with Bob on an overnight camp-out with the Rocky Mountain Hiking Club. Well, I wasn't much into mountain climbing, having grown up in a small town on the plains of Kansas. Bob was a great hiker, though, and skier in the winter, so I could hardly object to his inviting Marilou to go on the overnight. She loved to hike too. She'd grown up in Ft. Collins and always had been a little bored that I wasn't into that sort of thing as much as she wanted. Although I presumed there would be a large group of hikers, I still wasn't happy about it, and as it turned out I indeed shouldn't have been happy!

The Monday morning after the hiking week-end, Marilou met me after my 9:30 class and said we had to have coffee at the Union—she wanted to TALK. Well, she talked alright! The hike had been for a very select group of couples—three to be exact. And there wasn't much hiking done. Bob had seemingly proven himself to be one of the world's great lovers, and Marilou was then and there pledging herself to Bob for eternity. I was crushed, of course, but after a few feeble attempts to win her back, I finally told both Marilou and Bob that their happiness was what was most important and gave them my blessing. (But what I felt was not a blessing mood!)

Added to my distress at loosing Marilou was a feeling of betrayal by Bob. He had been especially friendly with me that early fall, and just a week before the harvest dance he had actually suggested that we do an over-night camp-out on Jones Peak, just the two of us, about sixty miles from Denver. He had borrowed his folk's car then, too, and when he picked me up I saw that he had a couple of those plastic disks kids use to slide on the snow in the winter. When I remarked on this, he said there was a small glacier on Jones peak, and that it would be fun to slide on it. As it turned out, Jones Peak was not on the usual sightseer's list of places to go. We drove miles off the highway before we camped. We took little more than a single-lane rut leading to the open meadow where the glacier neared its termination. Bob suggested we slide before we set up camp (sleeping bags and cooking stuff). I assumed he knew what we were doing, so I took a sliding disc over to the glacier—actually little more than unmelted snow on a rather steep slope. In the early twilight from where we were, it looked as though the snow-ice ended at a small stream and grassy meadow at the bottom, maybe a couple of hundred yards from where I took off.

Bob was standing by me when I pushed off, but for some reason he didn't start to slide. It was only a few seconds before I could see ahead that indeed the glacier did not come to a benign termination at the meadow, but that there was a definite drop-off. Fortunately, the snow was mushy from the warmth of the summer and fall sun, and I was able to stop my descent by sticking my leg out and jamming my heel into the snow. By the time I got myself stopped, I was nearly to the drop-off, which actually was at least twenty or thirty feet down to some very nasty, jagged rocks. Had I gone over the edge, I undoubtedly would have been killed.

Quite shaken, I managed to ease myself to the edge of the snow and ice and yelled at Bob, who was still standing at the top, telling him not to come. At the time, I felt only thanks that I'd managed to stop and that Bob hadn't started at the same time that I had. But now as my plane carried me over eastern Kansas, I began to wonder why he hadn't begun to slide when I did. He obviously knew the place because he had had no trouble finding the little lane off the highway that led to our camping spot. So why had he planned to slide on an obviously dangerous slope? Dangerous indeed! Lethal was a better term! He was an experienced skier and climber and should have known what a foolish thing it was to do. Of course, at the time I had had no suspicions, but now in retrospect, in view of Bob's subsequent less than admirable behavior by taking my girl away from me, I began to have some very disturbing thoughts. I kept telling myself that I was being irrational, but I couldn't fend off that little voice in the back of my head asking, "Why, why?"

Well, the rest of the flight was spent mulling over the events of the rest of that school year. After a bit, when I realized that I wasn't going to win Marilou back, I had started to date again. But it was all pretty much a matter of putting up a front. I didn't enjoy the dating, and I expect my dates didn't either. It wasn't until graduation was over and I went home for a summer job in a lumberyard that I began to get myself pulled together. Then in the fall, the challenge and the new environment at Yale took care of my broken heart, and I was able to handle Marilou's visit to me the next year in New Haven with real eclat.

As we began the descent into Stapleton International Airport in Denver, I shook off the malaise which had engulfed me as I had allowed myself to think back to those unpleasant times twenty-five years ago. By the time I had gotten my bags, rented a car, and picked up maps to get me through Denver and the new freeways that had been built in that megalopolis since my days in Colorado, I was looking forward to meeting old classmates with considerable pleasure. All except Bob Wexler, that is. But even that event had a certain fascination...like looking at a cobra about ready to strike and being unable to jump out of the way. Ah, Senator Wexler! You son-of-a-bitch!

CHAPTER 2

It was mid-afternoon when I arrived at the registration desk in the Student Union at the University. A big lounge had been turned over to our class, and it was immediately evident that the committee had gone all-out. There were several large bouquets of fresh flowers, and a table had been set up in one corner where punch, cookies, and bite-sized sandwiches were being dispensed with a lavish hand. It took me a moment to recognize the woman at the registration desk. Amanda Forsythe had always been good looking, and even in college she had had that patina that results from an affluent back-ground. But now in her late forties she was absolutely smashing! It took her longer to recognize me than it had taken me to recognize her, but another woman at the table did recognize me, probably because she had the list of preregistrants in front of her. She called out, "Donald Moffett, how good to see you!"

At that, Amanda jumped up, and coming round the end of the table, she gave me a hug, adding, "Oh, we so hoped you'd come!"

This gave me a warm feeling. At the same time, I was trying to place the other woman who had recognized me, an embarrassing situation. Then I saw that everyone had name tags pined to their dresses, so I recognized the poised, svelte woman as having been a mousy, insecure classmate who had figured not at all in my college experience. I shook hands with her, thinking that was the least I could do since she had recognized me. I hoped that she hadn't noticed that my eyes had first slithered to her name tag. Then Amanda was saying that Marilou had been looking for me and would be back in just a few minutes.

Having gotten my own name-tag, and Amanda's attention having being diverted to a new registrant, I decided to mix, my eyes focusing first on name tags and then on faces. It's amazing what twenty-five years can do to people. It seemed as though the drab ones, usually the grinds who made the dean's list each semester, had blossomed into well-dressed, out-going, poised, attractive people. On the other hand, when one grossly overweight man lumbered up to me and shook my hand as I looked at his name tag, I was shocked to see that he was Ken Hawkins. He had been one of the campus jocks, one of the shining lights of the hiking club, and actually had been on the infamous week-end "outing" that had marked the termination of my relationship with Marilou.

I could think of nothing to say other than, "Are you still climbing mountains?" though in view of his physical condition it was obvious that mountains of food were all he mastered these days. He laughed rather ruefully and indicated that he was much too busy to do any of that sort of thing anymore.

The senior prom queen, now a good fifty pounds heavier than she was on prom night, and with bleached hair, too much make-up, and looking really quite dowdy, remembered me (with the help of my tag), probably because she was a sorority sister of one of the girls I'd dated after the break-up with Marilou. We had barely exchanged pleasantries when I felt a hand on my arm, and there was Marilou herself.

In view of the various changes I had just observed in some of my former classmates, I had had some misgivings as to what Marilou might look like. Well, for the second time, I had that jab of something like pain or pleasure in my solar plexus, and at that point a very unwelcome feeling it was indeed! Marilou had added a few pounds also, but in all the right places. She was dressed conservatively but in excellent, elegant taste. Her hair, always naturally curly, was just beginning to show some gray but was exquisitely coiffed. Those big, baby-blue eyes behind the long, dark lashes that had sent me into paroxysms of unrequited desire as an undergraduate were looking at me intently, and for a moment I thought Marilou was going to cry. She reached up and gave me a moist kiss on the mouth and then said something to the effect that she was glad I had come. I was much too befuddled to remember exactly what her words were, but the sound of her voice, like some infernal time machine, took me back twenty-five years. I wanted to grab her in my arms and do then and there what I had never allowed myself to do when we were dating (but what Bob Wexler had allowed himself to do on that over-night!). However, at the same time, I experienced the old feeling of rejection and anger that had been so painful during that long-ago winter.

But like the phone conversation, we both turned cool and detached, exchanged pleasantries, told each other how well we looked, and asked a few questions about our present status in life. Marilou had obviously read the brief biographical sketch I had sent, and she very properly asked about my children. I had already determined that she had no diamond on her left hand, so my questions were related solely to her career. She indicated that she had a very responsible position in the University library and was pursuing a successful career on the side as a short-story writer for a number of popular women's magazines and was working on a novel. It was obvious that I had made no mistake in evaluating the quality of her clothes! I could almost see price tags in high three figures on the dress. And she wore a very elegant necklace that surely didn't come with cereal-box coupons. For a moment, I found myself regretting my action back there twenty-four years ago in New Haven. But that was absolute nonsense, and I told myself that I had to get myself under control, and right then!

A buffet supper followed by dancing to an orchestra had been planned for the evening's entertainment. The orchestra had been instructed to play music from our college days. Marilou was saying that she and Amanda hoped that I would join them at their table. This brought me back to reality, and having agreed to meet them at six-thirty, I went to check into my room.

A whole floor of the Union Building had been reserved for our class, so it was very convenient. The Union Building had been constructed after our days on campus. It was almost a city in itself, offering food services of various kinds, barber and beauty shops, bowling alley, book-store, gift shop, catering services, conference rooms, lounges, and a whole wing which was operated as a hotel for University guests.

The room was large and well appointed. Realizing that I was very tired, I threw myself on the bed and unexpectedly fell asleep almost immediately. But my dreams were miserable. I was back on campus as a student again, hunting for Marilou and finding her in a parked car necking with Bob Wexler. He was very fat, though, like the man, Ken Hawkins, I'd briefly talked to earlier—very unappetizing indeed. And Marilou just looked at me and said to go away so she could climax.

At that point, I woke up and realized it was time to get cleaned up for dinner. I found myself showering, shaving, and brushing my hair with unusual care. I was annoyed that my suit was wrinkled, something that normally didn't bother me very much, and I was particularly disturbed that my middle felt so uncomfortable as I pulled my belt in a notch tighter than I normally wore it. I took five minutes trying to get a decent shine on my shoes, and retied my necktie three times before getting it just so. Lucille would have been amazed, a fact that occurred to me and which caused me to experience a pang of guilt, for what I wouldn't admit to myself. So at six-twenty-nine I presented myself at the entrance to the handsome room where the buffet was set up.

Tables for four or six were arranged around a central dance floor, somewhat like a cabaret. Amanda and Marilou were already there, Amanda resplendent in a floor-length sheath of some sort of shimmering black material, and Marilou in a white tailored pant suit with sequins ornamenting all the places I didn't want to be caught looking at. After exchanging greetings, we went into the buffet and filled our plates. At Amanda's suggestion, we took a table as far as possible from the stage where the orchestra would be playing later. I assumed from this that the women wanted to spend the evening talking rather than dancing. I wasn't too sorry, because I assumed that my prowess on the dance floor probably had suffered greatly from decades of little practice. Furthermore, the prospect of holding Marilou in my arms on a dance floor filled me with misgivings—a mixture of anticipation, embarrassment, and guilt.

Although our plates were filled with delicious food, none of us seemed to be very hungry. I had had another attack of that stab in my solar plexus when I first caught sight of Marilou in that white, sequined outfit. I doubted, however, that the women's seeming lack of appetite was due to the sight of me with my thinning hair and the tightly belted paunch that was defying being camouflaged by my buttoned suit-coat.

Conversation was at first sporadic. Careers, comments about classmates who had returned, and in the case of Amanda and me, families. Amanda was now married to a man who was an editor on the Denver Post. He had also dealt in oil leases before the oil bust of the 80's, and obviously her life-style continued to be one of affluence comparable to that with which she had grown up. But after a bit, awkward silences ensued, and I had the definite feeling that both women were trying to broach some difficult subject but couldn't quite bring themselves to start. I had a good idea that it would have do with our past. Not being one to avoid meeting a problem head on, I decided to make what I hoped would not be a fatal leap.

"I miss not having Jake here. I hope it is not too painful for you, Amanda, to talk about it, but I never knew just how he was killed. I read a notice in the alumni magazine of his dying in a skiing accident. But there were no details."

The minute I'd said this I was sorry. It sounded so clinical and uncaring. But much to my relief, Amanda immediately seemed to relax. She, and to some extent Marilou, talked for the next fifteen minutes, or maybe more, giving me no chance to put in a word edgewise. Amanda began.

"It's been so long since it happened that sometimes I think it must have been two other people. But then I'll admit that the hurt is still there—actually so many hurts. They don't really go away, you know; they just bury themselves."

I found myself nodding agreement a bit too forcefully, and a glance at Marilou found her nodding also. Amanda continued.

"It was all so unnecessary, really. Jake was no skier. He'd gone skiing with Bob a few times, but he didn't really like it and could hardly keep up more than a hundred yards or so before he fell down. After graduation, Jake went home for the summer to get things organized at the farm, and we were to be married in October. But then his mother developed cancer and had to be operated on in September, so we postponed the wedding to December. I was upset by this, of course, and Jake drove up to campus the last week of October to be with me for a long weekend. I'd enrolled in some graduate courses, just to put in the time 'till the wedding. Well, unfortunately, Friday was my sorority's State Day so I was going to be tied up that night. But we four were going to go to an all-University fall dance Saturday night, and there were other plans for Saturday and Sunday. We four, Jake and I and Marilou and Bob had lunch together Friday—remember Marilou? It was then that Bob suggested that since I'd be busy Friday evening, he and Jake ought to go to the mountains for a camp-out. He said he'd heard of a neat place on a mountain called Jones Peak where there was a little glacier, and maybe he could give Jake one last skiing lesson. He said it wasn't like the big Alaskan glaciers, of course, but there was ice and snow that didn't melt away in the summer."

Marilou chimed in.

"I remember that only too well! I'd planned to be with Bob that evening, and there he was, suggesting a camp-out with Jake without even saying he was sorry to break our date. I was pretty teed off!"

Amanda didn't seem to hear Marilou. Her mind was back twenty-five years before.

"So they went to this Jones Peak. It was way off the road somewhere—I've never been there and wouldn't go there for a million dollars. But according to what Bob told us, the boys put on the skis which Bob had brought along, and Jake started down this slope of snow which covered the ice of the glacier. Bob said they could see the meadow at the end of the slope, and as Jake started down Bob said he yelled at him to not go too fast and to remember how to stop. But that is what has always seemed strange to me, because Bob knew Jake couldn't handle himself that well on skis. Stopping usually meant falling down for Jake. But of course, maybe it didn't seem very important. There had been an early snow at the high altitude, and Bob said it looked as though the slope of snow just leveled out into a meadow where the stream that came off the glacier had already frozen over. It was late in the afternoon and getting rather dusk already, so they didn't see that..."

During this account of Jake's tragedy, I felt every muscle in my body tightening up. When I interrupted, I am sure that my mobile face must have exhibited a maximum number of emotions. I think I may have shouted.

"But there was a drop off of thirty feet, with rocks below! And Jake didn't stop and was killed when he went over the edge!"

Both women looked very startled, and Marilou said, "But you said you didn't know anything about how it happened!"

Whatever my face had displayed before, I am sure now it was one hundred percent grim.

"I don't think that Jake was killed by accident!"

"But that's impossible!" Amanda was white and shaking.

"Jake was terribly banged up. I saw his body at the mortuary. He skied off that ledge! Bob told us. Oh, God, it was awful." And she covered her face with her hands as if to blot out what she must have experienced.

Marilou's eyes were wider than I'd ever seen them, and if I hadn't been so wrapped up in the drama at hand, I probably would have dissolved in a puddle on the floor right there. But sex was far from my thoughts at that moment as I grimly continued.

"Listen to me! Bob Wexler knew that glacier well. A week before that harvest dance at the first of our senior year, Bob took me on an overnight to Jones Peak. I didn't ski at all, so he didn't use that ruse. But he took a couple of those plastic disks the kids use in the winter to slide down snow banks. It was late afternoon when we got there, and it does indeed look as if the glacier just ends in a gentle slope into the meadow below. I figured Bob knew the slope. He certainly had known how to find the godforsaken place! He said something about our racing to the bottom, and I shoved off. It was only a few seconds though before I could see that there was a drop off. I was able to stop myself because the snow was still soft from summer and fall sun, but I was almost to the edge before I did get myself stopped. I had one sore leg and ankle for days from it. I looked back, thinking Bob might be about to go over, but he was still standing at the top. I was so relieved that he hadn't been killed and that I hadn't either that I didn't question anything. Anyway, why should I have? We were the best of friends. Especially that fall Bob had been unusually friendly, like suggesting the over-night. So you see? I think Bob knew exactly what he was doing when he sent Jake down that slope. The new snow would have made it faster than the mushy stuff I slid on, and he knew that when Jake went over the edge he'd be killed! I think it was murder!"

Both women were tense. Amanda was as white as a sheet, and Marilou was batting her big blue eyes so fast that I wondered if they might not cramp or something.

Finally Marilou managed to gasp out a "But why?"

My answer seemed to evolve as I spoke, with little or no forethought. But I guess the ideas had been there all along.

"Well, it was just a week after Bob took me to Jones Peak that he moved in on you, Marilou. He had tried to get me out of the way, but when that failed, he just had to do it the conventional way. I always figured that he had the hots for you, the way he used to watch us when we were dancing or necking in the car. And now hearing Amanda's story, I think that later Bob decided he had developed the hots for Amanda, and having failed the first time with me so he could get at you, Marilou, he knew just how to pull it off the second time. Amanda, how long was it after Jake was killed that Bob moved in on you?"

Amanda wiped her eyes with her napkin before answering.

"Well, I didn't consider it moving in, as you call it, but now that I think about, it I suppose it was. It was such a confused, distressful time. Bob seemed to be awfully cut up by it all. He kept saying that it was all his fault for letting Jake ski the slope. And he seemed to be so very sorry for me. He really got me through the first grief period. And Marilou was wonderful, too."

Amanda reached across the table and took Marilou's hand.

"She and Bob included me in all sorts of things, not giving me a chance to grieve alone. Then Bob started taking me places without Marilou, but I assumed it was with Marilou's permission."

Marilou looked grim as she withdrew her hand and almost hissed her retort.

"Well, at first it was, but later on I began to get the picture. I knew how Bob had, as Don says, moved in on me. I'll admit that at the time I'd actually been flattered by the maneuver. So when I saw the same operation going on with you, Amanda, it came as no surprise when Bob broke the happy news to me that he had fallen madly in love with you, and why didn't I go back to Don."

Amanda shook her head and obviously was laboring to get herself under control.

"I really felt so guilty at the time, but Bob was so, oh, you know, persuasive and attentive..."

Marilou interrupted, her voice hard and bitter.

"Tell me about it! I remember how I felt when he told me how I was the greatest thing that had happened to him and he couldn't wait to get me into the sack. Oh, it all came back this afternoon when I saw Ken Hawkins, the slob! I'm sure he was in on it with Bob to get that overnight set-up so that Bob could pledge his enduring love to me in the confines of his sleeping bag!"

All this candid confirmation of what I had suspected twenty-six years ago was embarrassing me considerably. At the same time, I was appalled at the direction this conversation had taken the three of us. A long silence ensued, and then Amanda spoke.

"Don, we should explain to you just why we so much wanted to talk to you—why Marilou called you to urge you to come to the reunion. As a matter of fact, this reunion was partly my idea. It was the only way I could figure to get the three of us together. And there are some other things, too. As you know, I was married to Bob Wexler for several years, during which time I had ample opportunity to figure out how he operated. After he broke up with Marilou, Marilou and I didn't have anything to do with each other, naturally. But a couple of years ago we ran across each other in Denver, and over some disgustingly rich desert at the D.and F. tea room, we realized that we should be the best of friends, as we had been many years before. We had both been shafted by that bastard, Bob Wexler. As we talked, we began to get things sorted out as to what his real motives in all this had been. By then he was married to Jessamin VonBronigan and was serving his first term in the U.S. Senate. That Wexler charm had gotten to the voters just like it had to us."

Amanda stopped talking and tried to make a stab at her food, which by now was quite cold. Marilou took up the chronicle.

"You see, it turns out that it wasn't our womanly charms or our virginity he was after, it was our fathers."

My rejoinder was one of bafflement. "Come again?"

"You remember," Marilou continued, "my father had a law practice in Ft. Collins, and he had one younger man as a junior partner and a couple of clerks working for him. Well, almost as soon as Bob and I started going together, Bob began to ask me about the possibility of his getting in with Dad when he had finished law school. Of course I thought that would be wonderful, but after Dad met Bob he informed me in no uncertain terms that we could forget that idea. Dad didn't like Bob at all. Dad was a sharp man and a great judge of people, and I think that he knew Bob was a shifty liar right from the start. I finally relayed that information to Bob as tactfully as I could, not about his being a shifty liar, of course. I still didn't believe Dad, but I knew Dad meant it about not taking Bob in with him. It wasn't long after that that Bob began to play up to

Amanda. I finally recognized the tactics as being the same ones he had used while I was going with you, Don. So then after Jake was killed and Amanda was alone, I wasn't at all surprised to be dumped. As you know, Amanda's Dad was in that big law firm in Denver—he's retired now, of course. That situation had a lot more potential than my dad's little firm in Ft. Collins had. It was all very calculating, but it never occurred to me that Bob would resort to...to murder, in order to achieve his ends."

Amanda had given up any pretense of eating.

"You want to know something? I had thought of it, after I got to know the lout. Oh, he was the ideal lover and courted me in all the proper ways. His approach was much more subtle than it had been with Marilou. He didn't suggest we sleep together till months after Jake's death."

Then realizing just what she had said, Amanda blushed and put her hand over her mouth.

But Marilou showed just how much she had matured and of what *savior-faire* she was capable.

"Don't sweat it, Amanda. Don, I am sure, figured out that Bob had, as they say, taken my virginity on that camp-out the weekend after the harvest dance." Then turning those luscious blue eyes to me, she added, "If you hadn't been so honorable in our relationship, I probably wouldn't have succumbed to Bob's advances. You know, I always sort of wondered why you never tried to go all the way. We both knew that Amanda and Jake were sleeping together whenever they could arrange it. I was too dumb to realize that it wasn't a lack of masculinity on your part—just a rigid code of ethics as you saw it."

I was quite speechless at the candor. But I needn't have worried about the conversational ball's being knocked into my court. Amanda was ready to take up the volley.

"My dad wasn't very much taken with Bob Wexler either, but he and Mom felt so sorry for me because of Jake, and they were glad that there was another man in my life. During his last year in law school, Bob was taken on in Dad's firm as a clerk, and then after we were married, he was made a junior partner.

But pretty soon Dad began to see what he was like. Dad's big firm had always had a fine reputation, not only as to its competent lawyers but as to its integrity. Bob Wexler began to get involved in some practices that were on the shady side, and when Dad called him on the carpet, he told Dad to stop being such a prude. He actually dared to give Dad some advice on a big case Dad was handling, suggesting some procedures or something that would have been strictly illegal. Well, Dad was furious and told Bob that if he weren't his son-in-law he'd kick him out of the firm then and there. Poor Dad was on the spot. He didn't want to hurt me, but he couldn't countenance the things Bob was trying to do."

Amanda stopped talking just long enough to shove her plate away from her in disgust. Then she continued.

"Dad needn't have worried. By then things were going badly at home. Right after our son was born, Bob lost interest in what he had always referred to as my heavenly, Venus-like body. And he wasn't interested in the baby at all. He was much too busy with his profession, and he was already getting into politics. Then came the real *coup de grace*. In his various maneuverings, Bob had gotten clubby with some of the lawyers in that big Bauer law firm. They were known in the legal circles as being absolutely ruthless, and nothing was too crooked so long as they won. That was right up Bob's alley. I'm sure he had tried to get into the firm, but for some reason—incompetence probably—he hadn't made the grade. Then Tillie Bauer came back from Europe where she'd been for a decade trying to establish herself as a sculpturist. She was a real looser any way you look at it. But there was lots of money back of her, so for a time she cut quite a swath in Denver's arty circles—Symphony board, Arts Council, that sort of thing. And the poor thing was ripe for the young Bob Wexler, five years her junior, charming, on the way up politically, and as crooked as her dad. I found out that she and Bob had been having an affair for some time, and by then I was completely disillusioned with him anyway, so, much to Bob's delight, I asked him for a divorce. My Dad was already wanting to boot him out of the firm, of course, and when he found out that I was through with Bob Wexler, he kicked him out then and there. Shortly after that, Bob and Tillie were married, and of course, he was taken into the Bauer outfit. Old man Bauer was so delighted to get his dog of a daughter married off and all the arty crowd out of his mansion that he would have agreed to anything. Actually, from what I heard from my Dad, old man Bauer had no reason to regret his new son-in-law's carrying on the family tradition of crookedness—at least till Tillie committed suicide."

This monologue was interrupted by some former classmates who by now had finished desert and were going out for a cigarette in the smoking lounge. Greetings were exchanged, and compliments to Amanda and Marilou for their part in arranging the reunion were expressed. The orchestra was getting their stands set up on the stage, indicating that the dancing would soon begin. The friends moved on, and Amanda collected her thoughts, saying, "Where was I?"

Marilou answered the question.

"You said Tillie had killed herself. But actually you are getting a little ahead of yourself. As I understand it, old man Bauer was anxious for his son-in-law to continue his climb in politics, and with the Bauer money and the Wexler knack for conning people, Bob finally got himself elected to the Senate. But about then things seemed to go bad with the Bauer fortunes. In spite of their tactics, they lost several important cases, and the firm was accused of some shady dealings having to do with the proposed damming of the South Platte River. My dad heard that Bob had terminated his connections with the Bauer firm because of his duties in the Senate, but it is my own opinion that he wanted to distance himself from the Bauer firm. He was trying to create a political image of Mr. Clean, not an easy task with his past record."

Marilou interrupted.

"Ah, but he didn't give up his legal practice entirely. One of the juciest clients the Bauer firm had was the VonBronigan

Group. Bob talked them into taking him on as their personal but unofficial legal council rather than working with Bauer. That didn't go over well with the Colorado business people in the know." I hated to admit that I had no idea what the VonBronigan Group was, but a political scientist is trained to get data.

"So what is the VonBronigan Group?" I've always been terribly impressed by any outfit that calls itself a group.

Amanda answered.

"We forget that you no longer are a Westerner. The VonBronigans are filthy rich, and probably as crooked as Bauer. They were heavily into mining, then into oil during the boom of the fifties and sixties. My present husband tangled with them several times and was the recipient of the underhanded way they operated. They branched out into a number of manufacturing ventures, and they own land all over the place. But Bob's becoming their in-house, lap-dog, legal advisor wasn't the end of it. There is a VonBronigan female also, the lovely Jessamin, debutante, Junior Leaguer, and viciously ambitious. She is ten years younger than Bob Wexler, but his political career was just what she wanted to crown the VonBronigan fortunes. However, there was just one problem—Bob's poor wife Tillie. Rumor had it that Jessamin was having an affair with Bob Wexler, by no means the first man to have bedded her. Knowing Bob, it was certainly a strong possibility. Then while Bob was in Washington the first year, Tillie, who hadn't gone East with him, was found dead in her Cadillac in the garage. The car's ignition was on, the gas tank was empty, and the garage was filled with carbon monoxide. Everyone assumed that she had killed herself because of Bob's affair with Jessamin or someone else, but between the Bauer's and the VonBronigan's money and power, there was very little about it in the papers. But you know how people talk. Since my dad's in the legal profession and since I'm an ex-wife of Bob Wexler, I was privy to all sorts of tales. Bob was in Washington when it happened, so no one seemed to think it could be anything but suicide. Now I'm beginning to wonder if he might somehow have engineered it so that a murder could look like suicide. I'd not put it past him, the bastard!"

The orchestra struck up a resounding rendition of an old Beatle song, which temporarily terminated conversation. After a bit, however, the orchestra settled into something a little less strident, which gave Marilou a chance to add to the tale.

"Of course, guess what! VERY shortly after Tillie died, Jessamin VonBronigan became Mrs. Senator Wexler. We will no doubt get to see her—all of her—at the banquet, adoring her beloved Senator husband as he tells us what noble plans he has for the great state of Colorado, to be possible, of course, only if he is reelected the state's Senator. But she'd better enjoy it while she can. He is in no way assured of being reelected. Tillie's suicide didn't do him any good, especially when he married Jessamin so soon afterwards. And his stands on the Platte River water thing and the expansion of the Denver airport are questionable in view of his connection with the VonBronigan interests. But let Amanda tell you about the campaign to get Bob defeated."

Amanda had gotten her second wind.

"My husband, as I told you, is with the Denver Post. The Post is very much against Wexler, and they are trying to dig up anything they can to help defeat him. I have a very strong personal grudge against my ex-husband, and I'd love to see him finally get his comeupance. My husband, Henry Davis, thinks I'm crazy, but I kept having a hunch that if we had this reunion and asked Wexler to be a speaker at the final banquet, somehow he might say or do something that would expose him for what he is. I had to work on Marilou quite a while to convince her to help get this thing organized. Of course, she has no love for Bob Wexler either. But now I am sure that this was a great idea! The information you have given us about Jones Peak and all that gives us ammunition we hadn't dreamed of!"

Marilou opened her eyes wide again, obviously having thought over Amanda's last remarks.

"Do you really suppose Bob somehow murdered or had someone else murder poor Tillie? Oh, I'm just sure he did. That scum-bag! But how can we prove any of this? It was all years ago, and the business about Jake would be only coincidence and based on just your word, Don. Oh, I didn't mean to put you down, but you know what I mean."

Marilou put her hand in top of my hand, and left it there for a longer period of time than was necessary, sending yet another stab of pain/pleasure through my gut.

Amanda was decisive. "Well, we are going to try to prove some of this. I didn't do all this work getting this reunion organized just to have the best information I could possibly have hoped for not bear some fruit. That orchestra is great, but time is awastin', as they say. I'm going to call Henry to be sure he's finished with the man he is meeting at our hotel, and then we're going to the hotel where we're staying and talk all this over with him. I guess I didn't tell you that Henry is here in town with me. He had to have dinner with some business associate or he'd have been here with us."

Marilou protested. "Oh, Amanda, let me have just one dance with Don, just for old times' sake!"

Amanda shot Marilou a rather disapproving look, but then capitulated.

"O.K., but just one. I'll go call Henry, and then there are some people I should talk to for a few minutes. I'll see you in the lounge." With that she swept off as Marilou led me out to the tiny dance floor. The orchestra was just striking up "Love Me Tender", a tune that had had a special significance for Marilou and me two-and-a-half decades before.

For the next little bit, it might just as well have been two-and-a-half decades earlier. Marilou had always been a beautiful dancer, and she could follow my somewhat erratic steps with consummate grace. We had always seemed to fit each other on a dance floor, and even with my extra, hateful, incipient paunch we still were, as they say, dancing as one. I was actually trembling and tried to disguise the fact by holding Marilou even tighter. It didn't help matters any to have Marilou turn her big blue eyes up to me and say, "We did have fun together, didn't we?" Then she put her head on my shoulder and squeezed my hand very tightly. Fortunately, just then Ken Hawkins and wife lumbered into us, almost knocking us down.

My annoyance at that was superceded by a wave of old hostility—Ken Hawkins, week-end camp-out, Bob Wexler, ergo desertion by Marilou. I stiffened. Marilou looked up at me questioningly, and I think she understood. Nothing more was said as we finished the dance in silence. We didn't go back to our table but went out to the lounge to await Amanda. As we walked off the floor, Marilou tentatively offered me her hand, but I didn't respond. We said nothing to each other, being occupied with our own thoughts. I had no idea what Marilou was thinking, but I was definitely confused and very upset. It had been a very long time since I had felt this way, and I didn't like it! Or did I?

CHAPTER 3

Marilou and I found a couple of big easy chairs in the lounge and sat in awkward silence for some time. Finally, Marilou looked at me and said, "I'm sorry, Don."

All I could reply was a lame, "I'm not sure what for, but it's O.K." Fortunately, Amanda bustled up just then, so further conversation was unnecessary. In a few minutes, we were in the parking lot getting into Amanda's Lincoln Continental. Marilou sat in front. I sat in miserable silence, sunk deep in the luxurious leather cushions of the back seat. But by the time we swung up to the entry of the hotel where the Davises were staying, I had gotten myself under control. Amanda handed the car keys to an attendant, and we went on into the pleasant lobby of the hotel. As we ascended to the sixth floor in the glass elevator, which gave a spectacular view of the atrium, Amanda was excitedly saying that she couldn't wait to tell Henry about our suspicions. I had to admit to a rising excitement also.

Henry Davis was a gem—a real top-drawer, smart, no-nonsense guy. Before Amanda could tell him what all the excitement was about, Davis had gone to the bar and was mixing us drinks—Scotch and soda for me, Martinis for Amanda and Marilou. He poured himself a Coors. Then, as we settled ourselves around a big coffee table, he sat back in his big armchair and asked, "Now, what is this all about? Amanda sounded absolutely incoherent when she called me. I gather that this wild idea of using a class reunion as a means of tripping up Bob Wexler is proving to be more of a success than I had hoped, not that I have any right to question my wife's judgment."

Then for the next half hour or so, Amanda, Marilou, and I went over pretty much all that had been said during our dinner conversation—our uneaten-dinner conversation. Henry Davis listened quietly, sipping his beer now and then and obviously registering every word that was spoken. He was a newsman through and through and didn't miss a trick. I very shortly had decided that we had a formidable ally in our campaign to discredit Senator Wexler, if such were at all possible.

When we had finished our stories, Henry fixed his dark brown eyes on me and spoke in an assured voice.

"I don't doubt but that your conjectures are correct. But to prove them as fact will be a damn hard job. Professor Moffett, would it be possible for you to stick around for a few days, even after the reunion is over?"

I didn't have to consider the suggestion for more than an instant. I was teaching summer term, but it didn't begin for a couple of weeks. For just a moment I considered the possibility of having Lucille come out to join me, but then for reasons, which I only later allowed myself to question, I ruled that out.

"Yes, I could arrange to stay, if it would be of any help. But what do you have in mind? And let's dispense with this Professor Moffett stuff. I'm Don, and if we are going to be partners in proving murder, you'd better be Henry."

"Good! I have ideas where you may be very helpful. And it's Hank. Only Amanda and my mother call me Henry. And now my dear conspirators, let's get down to business. The State of Colorado must not have this crooked opportunist represent it in the Senate for another term. He is not representing the people who elect him, only his selfish interests and those of the VonBronigans. He is anti-conservation, anti-controlled development, anti-civil rights, anti-anything-else-that's-for-the-common-good. I don't basically approve of dirty politics, but the kind of game Senator Wexler plays can be countered only by the most clever means. Understand, it is not a smear campaign I'm proposing, it is just exposing the truth. Getting the truth is our job. The Denver Post will take care of the rest of it."

Hank got up from his chair and went to the bar for another Coors. The rest of us refused refills of our drinks. Things were too tense to be muddied up with alcohol. Having returned with his beer, Hank settled down in his chair and began to lay out a *modus operandi*.

Reunion With Murder

"As soon as possible, Don, you and I will go up to the mountains and find this glacier on Jones Peak. I need to see for myself what the lay-out is. In the meantime, I'll have the boys down at the office get all the material that was printed at the time of Tillie Bauer's death. I guess I should say Tillie Wexler, shouldn't I? I think we should be able to find out from the Congressional Record whether or not Bob Wexler was really in Washington at the time of Tillie's death. Of course, if he didn't respond to roll call it wouldn't prove that he was not somewhere else in Washington, but we might be able to work on that from there. Now I want you all to suck up to the old bastard every chance you get. Don't let him for a moment suspect that you have any ulterior motives. Play the old-loves bit for all you're worth, girls. You know. No hard feelings—it was all for the good—didn't we have fun."

Marilou blushed at this last remark, no doubt remembering that she had said the same words to me on the dance floor. Hank didn't notice Marilou's discomfort as he continued.

"Don, you may well be a key player in this little charade. Be as old buddy-buddy as you can. Don't talk about Jake, but maybe you could get around to talking about your experience on the Jones glacier. See if you sense any discomfort on the part of Wexler when you are on the subject. But don't let on about your suspicions. I don't know how it will work out, but I'm hoping that somehow you can trip him up at some crucial point. We're going to have to play it by ear. Oh yes, and I think it would be best if Wexler didn't see you chumming with Amanda and Hank Davis. He'd become suspicious if he thought you were trying to get anything on him for the Henry Davis family. He can't be unaware of what I think of him personally, of course, and probably politically. But the Post hasn't started any overt campaign against him as yet. We've got to have facts first, cold, unassailable facts."

Then Hank seemed to withdraw from the rest of us, obviously thinking about the situation. Amanda and Marilou chattered excitedly about their roles as suggested by Amanda's husband. For my part, I sat silently, wondering if I'd be able to dissemble sufficiently to carry out Hank's directive. There always was the problem of my mobile features! And more to the point, would I be able to maneuver conversations in such a way as to get any damaging information from Bob Wexler? My musings were terminated when Hank jumped up and went to the phone that was sitting on the bar.

The first call was to someone connected with the Denver Post. Whoever it was was directed to go through the morgue and get every shred of information he could find about Tillie's presumed suicide. Hank next put in a credit card call to someone called Joe in Washington. It was pretty clear that Joe was someone close to him. Hank didn't even seem to feel it necessary to apologize for calling Joe late in the evening. When he gave orders to Joe, it was obvious that Joe was accustomed to taking orders from Henry Davis.

"I'll have my secretary call you first thing in the morning, about ten thirty your time. She will give you a date about five years ago. No explanation of what date. I want you to check the Congressional Record to see if Senator Robert Wexler answered roll call either on that day or on the next. That should be easy.....Yes, that's right. Now, the next job will test your usual ingenuity and charm. I'd like to know if Wexler made a plane reservation for a flight from Washington to Denver on that date, possibly even if Wexler had been discharging his senatorial duties during the day. He might have taken a night flight. Or he might even have taken a flight to some other city, say New York or who knows where, if he was covering his tracks. And, of course, he could have used an assumed name for that matter. It's usually the secretaries who have to do this sort of thing. ...Yes...You've got the idea, as usual. Good man!...Yes, as a matter of fact, I do. We think that Wexler may have been having a little thing with a secretary in his office at the time his wife comitted suicide. The woman probably thought she might have an inside track with her boss after his wife was no longer extant. But the secretary was left in the wings waiting for a non-existent cue when the Senator married a Denver socialite...You're wonderful, Joe. I hate having to spell everything out for people. You're way ahead of me...Yes, I think the woman might still work in Wexler's office. If she doesn't, track her down if you can. She may be willing to be indiscrete and give you some information, just to get even with her philandering boss...What?...Oh, her name is Anderson, Marvella Anderson. And I understand that she is quite a dish, so the task shouldn't be too distasteful or difficult for a man of your, ah, talents...Ah yes, that's my man! If we can get information from the marvelous Marvella it will save us having to get the information through legal sources from airlines and credit card people. That could be a real bitchy bore. And thanks again, Joe, for not asking me why I want this information. Not that you haven't probably figured it all out for yourself by now. So go back to whatever you were doing and give my regards to whoever may be waiting for you between the sheets. Bye now."

I was absolutely agape at this performance. Life in academe does not expose a political scientist to this sort of wheeling and dealing or whatever one could call it. Amanda took all this in stride, having given about as much attention to her husband's phone conversation as she would have had he been ordering out for a pizza. But I could see that Marilou had been more attentive to Hank's call than she had to what Amanda was saying. She was looking pretty impressed, I can tell you. It was like some episode from a police detective-type television show. I was wondering who this Joe was—no doubt some sort of James Bond character—when Hank made a partial explanation.

"When one has been in the newspaper business as long as I have, one has made some pretty valuable contacts. I've met a lot of interesting people, too. Joe and I worked together for a couple of years on the Washington Post before I came to Denver. He is in business for himself now."

I got the definite impression that Joe was never to have a last name as far as I was concerned. My expressions were probably registering some sort of quizzical reaction which Hank felt warranted a rejoinder.

"His business, since you are probably wondering, might be called an information service. He provides us with what we in the press refer to as an 'unnamed source'."

All I could think of saying was something to the effect that I was impressed. Hank chuckled.

"You'd be more impressed if you ever got to know him. He has never married, but I doubt if he has slept alone more than a dozen nights in his adult life." Then seeing that he had captured his wife's attention, he added, "But then, he has never had the good fortune to meet a woman like Amanda."

This last remark expressing marital felicity seemed to cause Marilou discomfort. She may have said that she had had enough romance for a life-time, but I doubted very much that she had really meant it. At any rate, she seemed to want to change the subject, and actually it was time to get down to the nitty gritty of what we were going to do next. Amanda was eager to have some definite ideas as to our next procedure.

"There's a brunch tomorrow morning at the Country Club. We think Bob Wexler probably will attend that since he has ordered a ticket. He undoubtedly thinks he can do some hot campaigning. After the brunch, buses take us on a tour of new campus buildings. Don, if you could make contact with Bob during brunch, maybe you could suggest having a drink with him sometime—for old time's sake, you know—and that would give you the opportunity to do whatever it is you will be able to do."

I felt like saying, "Thanks a bunch, Amanda. And just what the hell AM I going to be able to do?" I was finding these high powered, sophisticated people a bit daunting. We don't have very many of that type in the Political Science Department at DeMott University. Well actually, not any. For a moment I felt real warmth towards Marilou, another human being who also presumably wasn't moving in the fast lane all the time. But that implied that we were kindred spirits moving on our own more leisurely lanes, and I didn't feel comfortable about that either...not with Marilou's big blue eyes looking at me that way and those damn sequins winking at me from a number of provocative locations on that pant suit. Further consideration of my very human condition was interrupted by Hank's next remark.

"By tomorrow afternoon, Joe will possibly have some information for us from Washington. I've got to go back to Denver in the morning, and I'll have all the available information on Tillie Bauer's death by then. I'll be back here by six o'clock. Let's have a rendezvous up here at six before we go to the banquet at seven. We'll have a better idea of what we are up against. Of course, we'll encounter the Senator in full cry at the banquet tomorrow night, unless a bolt of lightening strikes him dead after his seventh lie in front of all you honorable people."

That seemed to close the subject of Bob Wexler. After a little casual conversation, Amanda said we were looking tired and she would take Marilou and me back to the Union Building. I shook hands with Hank Davis, the glass elevator bore us down to the nearly deserted lobby, and Amanda's posh Continental bore us silently back to campus.

We all were preoccupied with our own thoughts, and of course, the Continental's engine hardly gave us indication that it was running. It might as well have been one of those old-fashioned electric cars that the rich used to creep around in during the early part of the 20th Century. Only we weren't creeping, not with Amanda at the wheel! As Marilou and I got out of the car, Amanda suggested she pick us up the next morning to take us to the brunch at the Country Club. We agreed to leave the Union at ten o'clock.

Marilou and I hadn't said a word to each other until we got into the elevator. But the tension was such that I felt there must be a batch of treble-tuned wires running between us. If I reached up I maybe could twang them, play some infernal tune. And then I almost heard the tune we had danced to, "Love Me Tender."

Marilou was hunting in her little sequined bag for her room key as we got out of the elevator. She broke the silence.

"What's your room number, Don? I'm 426."

I was 430, so we got to her door first. It occurred to me that I hadn't shown a woman to her door since I was courting Lucille. Not that this should be any big deal. Just a 'Good-night'—'Nice being with you again'—'See you tomorrow.' But no! I had to make it a big deal. As Marilou turned the key in the door, I impulsively put my arms around her and gave her a hard, long kiss on the mouth. And the response was terrific. When we finally came up for air, Marilou sort of whispered, "Don't you want to come on in?"

At that point my guardian angel came to my rescue—late, but better late than never. Actually, it was what Marilou said that triggered my reaction. I don't really believe in guardian angels. But those were exactly the same words she had said when I had left her at the door of the hotel in New Haven twenty-four years ago. Only I hadn't kissed her that time. *Au contraire.* And I swear that my answer was exactly the same as it had been then. Talk about *deja vu!*

"No, my dear, it is too late for that."

And I am pretty sure my tone of voice and inflection matched that of the first time, because I was suddenly infused with the same feeling of anger and resentment I had experienced that other time long ago.

Marilou looked startled, as well she might, since I had taken the initiative in this ridiculous little episode.

"Oh, Don, it's only eleven o'clock, and Amanda isn't picking us up till ten."

But then she must have seen the look on my face.

"Oh, oh I understand. I misunderstood, I guess. I'm sorry. I'll see you in the morning."

Then she was gone, but the door didn't close quickly enough for me not to have seen the tears in her eyes—those big blue eyes behind the long, dark lashes.

I stood at the door for several minutes. Was I considering knocking and saying that we should go back to where I took her in my arms? My anger had subsided as rapidly as it had arisen. But I suddenly felt totally exhausted. This roller coaster ride my emotions were experiencing was hard to take. Then I found myself considering seeing if I couldn't get a plane out from Stapleton Field the first thing in the morning. That actually was my intent as I went on down the hall to my room. But by the time I'd unlocked my door, I was thinking of that other problem—the real problem—proving that Bob Wexler, the rat, was also a murderer, and thoughts of my splitting were forgotten.

As soon as I had gotten into the room, I made a dash for the phone. If I could just talk to Lucille I'd get this silly Marilou thing out of my system. But by the time I'd looked up Lucille's mother's number in Columbus and had dialed the thirty-one digits to activate the MCI credit billing, I realized that it was past one o'clock in Columbus. I hung up before the first ring.

As I got ready for bed, I tried to concentrate on my directive from Hank. How could I in any way compromise Bob Wexler if and when we got into conversation? Hell, compromise wasn't the word! Maybe the word was implicate. But we'd already implicated him. Get proof that he was a murderer, that was it. But how? After I was in bed and the light was out, my mind seemed to become some sort of mental pendulum. Bob Wexler—Marilou Baxter—Bob Wexler—Marilou Baxter—tick tock. Periodically an alarm would to go off in my head—stupid fool, stupid fool, stupid fool, ding, ding, ding. Then the pendulum would start again. Maybe it was the regularity of this that finally made me drift off into an uneasy sleep. I don't remember specific dreams, just vague impressions of snow banks ending in an abyss, somebody that looked like Peter Falk but whose name was Joe saying, "Sorry boss, but I didn't get you any information." And once I woke up hugging my pillow, with the distinct impression I'd been holding Marilou. Really, it was all too much for a middle-aged "polysci." professor from a conservative Midwestern university, happily married for twenty-

Oswald G. Ragatz

two years, and with two grown children! Too much, too much! It was no wonder that when I woke up in the morning I felt as though I'd climbed up Long's Peak, not that I've ever done that, of course, flat-lander that I am, but I can imagine. The Rocky Mountain Hiking Club had never had much appeal for me!

CHAPTER 4

I wasn't the only one who looked and felt like warmed over pizza the next morning. Marilou was waiting under the marquee at the front entrance of the Union Building when I got there. The dark circles under her eyes were more than too-much eye shadow. We said good morning to each other with as much warmth as though we had just been introduced to each other in some receiving line. Further need for communication was preempted by the arrival of Amanda's Continental. Actually, Amanda didn't look much better than did Marilou or I, for reasons which immediately became apparent the minute she swung out of the drive.

"I was so excited about this Wexler thing that I couldn't get to sleep for hours. Henry and I talked a while about it after I got back from taking you to the Union, but he didn't loose any sleep over it. He's so cool and in control. It's wonderful being married to him. I suppose I owe Bob Wexler a vote of thanks for making me appreciate what I have in Henry Davis. I might just have assumed that all men are like Henry if I hadn't married that bastard Wexler first. I just can't believe that I lived with the creep for five years! It's a wonder I married again. For a while I assumed that all men must be like Bob. Thank God Henry came along and talked some sense into my head. And he has always been so wonderful with Robbie—that's my son by Bob Wexler. Robbie and Liz, Henry's and my daughter, are absolutely devoted to their father. Henry, of course, adopted Robbie just as soon as we were married. Sometimes I ask myself why I have been so lucky in life. First my neat parents, and then Henry and my children. We'll ignore the five years out with that snake, Bob Wexler."

I got the distinct impression as I watched Marilou from the confines of the rich leather of the back seat of the Continental that this testimonial to marital bliss was causing her considerable discomfort. It was the same reaction I'd noticed the night before in a similar situation. I wondered why Marilou had not been able to surmount the trauma of Bob's desertion—and my rejection when she came back to New Haven. She is a very attractive woman—oh yes, indeed she is! Too damn attractive. We all manage to get past the disappointments and traumas of broken love affairs. Why hadn't she? And then I remembered my own confusion of the night before, and I had to tell myself, "Like hell we do!"

Marilou had steered the front seat conversation to something to do with seating plans for the banquet, which seemed to be one of her committee's tasks. This gave me time to pursue my thoughts about Marilou. Of course, the episode at her door the night before was foremost in my mind when I suddenly came up short with the question, "Why was Marilou staying at the Union Building at all?" She worked for the University library, so presumably she would live in town near the campus. She could, of course, commute from Denver. It wasn't all that far actually. Probably it was just more convenient to stay at the Union where the action was. But still... For some reason the question remained in my mind.

Amanda and Marilou soon were back on the major issue—Bob Wexler. Amanda was leaving no conversational gaps.

"Henry left early this morning to drive back to Denver. When he gets a lead on anything, it's full speed ahead and damn the torpedos. I'm sure that by now he has read all the material on Tillie's death, probably has tracked down the coroner who was on the case and contacted any household staff that might have been working for the Wexlers at the time. Rest assured, his friend Joe (again no last name, just Joe) will have all sorts of tidbits for Henry by the time we meet at 6 o'clock. Actually, I've never met Joe. I think maybe Henry is afraid Joe might seduce me or something, judging from what Henry says about Joe's success with the women. But he is a real operator, with the most amazing network of, how should I put it?—information sources in Washington. I have a suspicion that Joe's tactics employ a mix of sex and blackmail, and he seems to have a shrewd understanding of the weaknesses of human nature. But some of Henry's best exposés for the Post have been the result of the information gleaned by the ineffable Joe."

I wondered if perhaps even Amanda didn't know Joe's last name. These comments about Joe were delivered as Amanda swung the Continental into the broad driveway leading to the porte-cochere of the Country Club. The young man who took the car keys was rewarded by Amanda's dazzling smile, and thanking her, he called her Mrs. Davis. This certainly was a milieu unfamiliar to most of us who spend our lives in a small Midwestern town teaching political studies or what ever at a modest sized university. But I thought I might be able to get used to it real soon, given the chance. A most unlikely possibility!

As we were going up the steps of the club, Amanda reminded us that we shouldn't be together, in case we would encounter Bob Wexler. I assumed that did not apply to Marilou and me, but at the moment it was debatable whether or not either one of us wanted to be with the other. So we all split up as we went into the entry.

Again the planning committee had gone all-out. I had winced at the cost of the reunion, but as I proceeded into the solarium and saw the spread, I understood. I greeted a number of old acquaintances as I worked my way toward the brunch buffet. Ken Hawkins was at the trough, his plate piled high with all the usual breakfast items plus a number of things from the steam table that were strictly high calorie lunch or dinner fare. He was at the same time in animated conversation with Babbs Buehler, erstwhile prom queen, whose plate pretty much matched Ken's. Well, they were getting their money's worth at the buffet, a rationale which I actually understood myself. But at this particular moment, influenced no doubt by my recent concern about my waistline, I had just completed my modest selection of low calorie breakfast items when someone behind me grabbed my shoulder, almost causing me to spill my food on the floor. Before I had a chance to recover my balance and look around, I heard Bob Wexler's hearty voice.

"But how can you think of food when an old friend is waiting to say hello! How are you Don, old buddy? This is the moment I've been looking for ever since the announcement of the reunion crossed my desk.!"

I personally questioned the veracity of that last statement as every word dripped insincerity! But I understood his success with the electorate. For that moment the room seemed to have only two people in it, and I had the sole attention of the charismatic Senator Wexler.

I couldn't help but notice that his plate was even more sparsely decorated with food than was mine. Obviously this Spartan approach to food had paid off handsomely. Bob was tall for our generation, a good six feet, but that disgusting thirty-six inch waistline and the broad shoulders (possibly a bit padded?) made him look even taller. There wasn't a touch of gray in his hair, but I didn't remember that his basic hair color had been that notably auburn. It was the reddish highlights that cast a bit of suspicion in my mind. The eyes were the same, a hard blue, and now I remembered that they had seemed to have no depth and were just a bit protuberant. Bob finally relaxed the vice-like grip on my shoulder as I managed to turn around and face him squarely.

"Don, my friend, I've got a table over here in the corner where we can talk. You've got to sit with me! Marilou will just have to wait to practice her charms on you!"

This was said with a nod to a small group of people at the end of the buffet where Marilou was watching us intently. As soon as she saw Bob look toward her, she turned to her companions and immediately engaged in animated conversation.

"Tsk, tsk, that little lady surely isn't still carrying the torch for either of us, is she? But she IS looking in the pink as they used to say, almost as handsome as my classy ex-wife over there. Too bad she and her old man were such Puritans! I might have enjoyed walking into the sunset of maturity with a doll like that.

Reunion With Murder

But you haven't met my Jessamin! Now THERE's one gorgeous female! She will be with me at the banquet. Anticipate, friend, anticipate!" During all this palaver, Senator Wexler had been dexterously piloting us to a table by a window overlooking the second hole of the golf course.

Lucille and I try to stay on a low-sodium diet for the most part, but it occurred to me that the salt I was having to mentally sprinkle on each of Bob's remarks could probably raise my blood pressure fifty points. That pressure had already been considerably disturbed by my encounters with Marilou.

The Senator was in full cry—wired, as they say, and at high voltage. I couldn't help but wonder if he would ever stop talking long enough to eat any of the food on his plate.

"It's been too long, my friend, too long! But it HAS been one hell of an exciting life. I'd not have wanted to miss a minute of it. Now if I can just pull off this election to my second term in that august body, the U. S. Senate, I've got so many plans for really great things that can be accomplished that I can't count them! I say, I hope your life has been as rewarding as mine has been.

I managed a half dozen words of no consequence while Bob took two quick bites from his unbuttered toast. But I'm not one of your rapid-fire talkers, and so I lost control of the conversation before I'd made one complete sentence.

"Impressive! Yes, impressive! I read your bio. in the reunion booklet, and it's obvious those brain cells of yours that were always in overdrive have made a good life for you. There were a number of times your brain cells were mighty useful for me, if you recall. I still remember your trying to explain Thorstein Veblen's theories to me. I do believe you succeeded in getting some of the ideas pounded into my head. I certainly have enjoyed proving some of the points he made regarding the behavior of the leisure class! What was the name of his book, 'Theory of the Leisure Class'?"

Well, he remembered the title of the Veblen classic, but he obviously had missed the point of Veblen's theories. So much for my efforts, though I had to admit that he had given me credit for trying to help him. I remembered well cramming with Bob for the Veblen exam. Actually, the class notes had summaries of Veblen's theories as set forth in several of his books—MY class notes that is, not Bob's. He'd not bothered or had cut classes when our professor was lecturing on Veblen. Bob didn't know it, but he shouldn't have mentioned that episode to me now. It merely had gotten me to thinking of the many occasions when my notes had rescued him, to say nothing of his sitting next to me during exams so he could crib. I didn't object because he was my friend, so I thought, and I didn't have so many friends that I could afford to be choosy. There was one notable occasion when I had shown Bob an article I'd run across in an obscure journal. I'd figured he might get an idea or two from it or perhaps a quotation. But he copied it word for word and turned it in as his own. I didn't know about this till some time later—after he had gotten by with it. I was angry that time, but he told me to stop being such a Puritan, the same term I now realized that he had just used in reference to Amanda and her father. I was hardly listening to Bob as he rattled on about his successful career and how important it was that he be reelected to the Senate. I just kept resurrecting incidents of his dishonesty during those undergraduate years. Mostly I was castigating myself for having been so dumb or permissive in the name of friendship. If I were the honest person I considered myself to be, I should have blown the whistle on him.

But I did listen to him enough as he recounted his life's experiences to note that it had taken him at least an extra year to get through law school. I remembered that he had tried to get into Harvard Law School, but his undergraduate record certainly was not good enough for that. He had settled for the University of Denver Law School, and of course that had made it possible for him to work into Amanda's father's firm, first as a part time clerk and eventually full time.

But now the Senator jumped up and rushed over to some new-comers. After much hand shaking and back patting—well, more like banging—he returned to our table.

"Sorry to leave you, friend," Bob shouted, forgetting that he was now back to one-on-one and not having to communicate with a whole group of people. Then lowering his voice to a stage whisper meant to impress, he added, "That was John J. Hazelworth, president of Denver National. Very important man, very important. You remember him, don't you? Was president of the Betas."

Before I had to humiliate myself by admitting that I did not remember John J. Hazelworth, nor had I known very many Betas even by name, Bob was off again on a new tack. Before I managed to focus my whole attention on what he was saying, I had time to consider the fact that though neither of us had been able to afford belonging to a fraternity, obviously Bob even then had kept tabs on "the people who count." And it had seemingly paid off. But do people who count often resort to murder to achieve their high status in life? I couldn't remember Thorstein Veblen having commented on that particular facet of behavior of the leisure class. I'd have to look up his books when I got back to campus. It had been years since I'd given those theories much attention. But now Bob finally had my divided attention.

"I can say this to you because you have known me for so long. I don't need to tell you that my talents do not extend to deep philosophical thinking or to dealing with abstract social or economic theories. And I make no apologies for that. Many of my colleagues in the Senate are great politicians but are not particularly versed in the finer points of the social sciences. And even a politician needs some help in, how shall I put it? understanding the voters. The big scene, you know, the forces that make people think and act the way they do at any given moment. In other words, I need someone to evaluate my campaign from a professional, scientific standpoint. An egghead who will help me, ah, mold my constituents' thinking, convince them that what I want to do is what they want also. My own private think-tank, as it were. And I think you are just the man for that. I know you, I can trust you, and you would give real panaché to my campaign team. A real, live political science professor, a genuine egg-head who's written books and articles, know what I mean?"

I sat in stunned silence, while Bob actually turned his attention to his cold toast and tepid coffee.

The thoughts that raced through my head were definitely on fast forward. I couldn't possibly be a part of what obviously was a campaign built on covert motives, the VonBronigan interests and all that. But how impressive such an assignment would be back at DeMott University! It would look GOOD on my annual report to the University President. But what about my commitment to our own covert project of proving that the Senator had been a murderer? Ah, but such a post would put me in a position to get all sorts of information for Henry Davis! But what a dirty trick that would be! Would the end justify the means? What would Hank Davis think about all this—and Amanda—and Marilou? Wouldn't they think I'd sold out, betraying their confidences? Actually, I'd be a sort of double agent! Heady stuff! But I hardly thought I had talent for such a task.

All this self-questioning came to an abrupt halt as Senator Wexler fixed his slightly protruding blue eyes on me with a hypnotic stare.

"Now Don, I know that you're thinking." (Like hell he did! At least I hoped to God he didn't!) "I left out some of the important parts. Most of the important work you'd do would be through the coming summer, say three or four months at the most. I'll pay you fifteen thou. a month, and you can live in Colorado, either at the VonBronigan summer place above Evergreen, or in one of the penthouse suites in an apartment high-rise the VonBronigans own in down-town Denver. I'll have to go back to Washington in a day or so, but I'll be in and out all summer, drumming up votes."

Then, as he looked across the room to the table where Marilou was seated, facing us, Bob added with a leer, "and from the way Marilou Baxter is looking at you with those lovely blue calf eyes of hers, you could have an extra bonus. From what she told me when we were going together, there is quite a bit of unfinished business you need to take care of with that little lady! Now what more could a man want? Money, prestige, elegant housing, Colorado, and sex."

Fast forward no longer would describe my thoughts. It was strictly rewind speed, and then start over again. Only now were added money—in four months I'd make what I make all year—a life-style that I'd never be able to afford on my own; prestige and excitement; and Marilou? This last brought me up short. Of course not Marilou. I'd have Lucille come out to Colorado just as soon as she had her mother settled. Oh yes, and there was summer term. I was scheduled to teach a 200 course for underclassmen. But a junior colleague could do that just as well as I, and he would be delighted to have a summer-term appointment. Integrity, loyalty to Hank Davis and Amanda, those and other nuisance concepts were for the moment getting lost in a wave of pure venality. Maybe Lucille wouldn't want to leave her roses. Or maybe she wouldn't like the high altitude of Colorado. It was, after all, a mile high. Marilou? Oh no! What had happened to that long-ago resolve so admirably carried out in New Haven?

But then a nasty word put an end to my mental dithering: MURDER. In my mind's eye I could see a young Bob Wexler standing at the top of a snow bank looking down at me as I finally came to a shuddering and painful stop a few feet from death on the rocks below. And again in my mind I could hear Marilou's voice telling me, between sips of coffee, how she had fallen madly in love with Bob Wexler during that infamous overnight.

My mind was made up, but I wasn't going to give Bob Wexler an answer until I had a chance to talk it over with Hank and Amanda. "Bob, I'm really flattered. It IS an enticing proposition, I must say, not only the money and a chance for a summer in Colorado, but the opportunity for a real change of pace. But I'll have to see what arrangements I can make for my summer-term teaching commitments. I'll make some phone calls this morning. And I must talk to my wife, too."

At this last comment, Bob looked at me and sighed heavily. "Dear old Don, always the upright and honorable one. However, that's why I'm hiring you. Just don't miss an opportunity to take just a sip from the cup of love that Marilou is offering you. Take it from one who once had the pleasure of deep draughts of that heavenly elixir." I didn't need a reminder of that!

Bob Wexler had developed a command of the trite phrases, no doubt useful in campaign speeches. But the effect on me was one of nausea. It merely intensified my disgust with that whole shoddy episode of twenty-five years ago. I cringed at the memory of my speech about whatever made them happy would make me happy.

During the last few sentences, I could see Wexler's eyes sweeping across the expanse of the dining-room, his radar seeking out other important personages to buttonhole. His gaze locked in on a table where four well-dressed men sat. I fully expected to see a large card upright in the center of the table, RESERVED FOR MOVERS AND SHAKERS. He sprang up, ready for action. I'd seen the same demonstration of resolve many times on the football gridiron as the players came out of a huddle and dashed for their positions. The Senator did take time to grab my shoulder, however, causing me to spill my coffee.

"Think it over Don, old buddy. Maybe you can let me know tonight at the banquet after you hear my speech...AND meet my lovely wife." He laughed heartily at what must have been some private joke as he left me mopping up the spilled coffee. As Queen Victoria was reported to have said, we were not amused.

I watched Bob weave between tables and people returning to the buffet. Before he reached the four important looking men, he made a brief detour past Marilou. He stopped momentarily, said something to her that made her look over at me and then quickly look away. Then he loped on to his destination. I had the distinct impression that Marilou was very angry and quite embarrassed. I saw her excuse herself to her companions, and then she fled through the door leading to the lounge.

Having finished my meager breakfast and having just spilled the last of my coffee, I was at a loss as to what I would do next. It was a half hour before the bus was to take us on the tour of the campus. If I went to the lounge, I'd have to cope with the possibility of encountering Marilou. I saw Amanda at a table far from both mine and the one where Marilou had been sitting, but Amanda was off limits for the termination of Wexler's presence in the room. The decision was made for me, however, by the arrival at my table of a couple I had known fairly well in college. They had actually double-dated with Marilou and me on occasion.

They were at first rather reserved in their greetings. I suggested that they sit down, relieved not to be left alone in a room filled with happily chatting people. Ed finally made a remark that explained their diffidence.

"We saw you having breakfast with Senator Wexler. I suppose you were talking over old times. Or was it politics?"

"Now Bob," his wife remonstrated, "that's none of our business." But then she continued on a subject that definitely wasn't her business.

"We were a bit surprised that you seemed so cluby with Bob, remembering how he had taken your girl away from you twenty-five years ago."

Something in the tone of voice of both Ed and his wife caused me to think that they weren't overly fond of the Senator from Colorado. It occurred to me that I might as well begin to test my skills at being a double agent. (Did this mean I had already made up my mind to accept Bob's offer? The more rational part of my mind told me that it must just be a fishing expedition, just to see IF I could do it.)

"Oh, that. Well, Bob seems to believe in letting bygones be bygones." Then I hastily added, but not very convincingly, I'm afraid, "And so do I. That was a long time ago."

Ed's wife surreptitiously glanced at my left hand, no doubt to reassure herself that I indeed had recovered from my ill-starred college romance and was now happily married. If she had seen me last night at Marilou's door she might not have been so reassured. I felt impelled to continue.

"Actually, our conversation was mostly a monologue on the part of the Senator and dealt with his political campaign. I must say I found it a bit confusing. I wasn't up on Colorado issues. We in the Midwest are pretty unaware of regional conflicts other than our own. But as I thought about it, I hadn't gotten a very clear picture from Bob's conversation either. I must say it's a sobering experience for a political science professor to encounter the realities of grass-roots politics. We in academe are often criticized for having our own arcane vocabulary. But at least our terms have precise meaning, I hope. As I listened to Bob I was struck by the fact that he used ordinary, every-day vocabulary, but damned if I knew what he was saying. I do believe the words all have several different meanings as the politicians use them. When a politician says he wants this or that for the betterment of his constituents, I swear that what he probably means is that what he wants is something for the betterment of himself and the people who are funding his campaign."

The ploy worked. Maybe I did have talent for this sort of thing. For the next twenty minutes I was again on the listening end. It immediately became obvious that this couple was violently opposed to what they perceived to be many of Wexler's goals and motives. Their perception was based not on his campaign promises but on his record during his first term in Washington and on the VonBronigan connection. It was obvious that they did not consider the interests of that group (I guess it should be in capitals—GROUP) to be compatible with the best interests of the rank and file of Colorado citizenry. Their resentment and hostility were obvious. It all supported Hank's comments of the night before.

When it was nearly time for us to take the bus for the campus tour, Ed and his wife shook hands and said it had been fun talking with me. "To me," would have been more precise. But I was thankful for the encounter. I felt considerably more comfortable about our proposed vendetta against Senator Wexler than I had up to now. This is not to say that my mind was completely made up as to what my role would be. But when I'd think of a summer in Denver, expenses paid and a handsome salary to boot, like Don Quixote I would be ready to mount my Rocinante and charge off to tilt at windmills. My sense of moral rectitude was taking a real beating!

The remainder of the day was somewhat of a blur. The chartered buses took us to various buildings and other points of interest on the burgeoning campus. There were a few moments of nostalgia, at places where there had been occurrences of momentous emotional import, usually involving Marilou. That lovely lady was nowhere to be seen. Of course, she hardly needed a tour of the campus where she worked. Amanda was on hand part of the time, and we exchanged a few words, nothing more.

By four o'clock, when the tour was over and we were deposited at the Union Building, I was exhausted. Back in my room, I took off most of my clothes, thankful for air conditioning, and was asleep in minutes.

CHAPTER 5

The phone woke me up a little before five-thirty. It was Amanda saying that she would pick Marilou and me up at a quarter of six. This gave me very little time to take a quick shower, shave, and dress. There was no time this evening for special attention to my appearance. As a matter of fact, I was not nearly as interested in how I looked as I had been the evening before. As I waited for the elevator to take me to the lobby, I hoped that this indicated a termination of the unwelcome renewal of those old feelings for Marilou. I had to admit that my uncharacteristic concern for my appearance the night before had undoubtedly been prompted by a desire to appear attractive to Marilou.

However, my hope that my attraction to Marilou might be a passing aberration was futile. When I arrived at the entrance lobby, there was Marilou, resplendent in a floor-length gown of some sort of shimmering blue material that emphasized every tiny move she made. The dress seemed to be held up in the most tenuous fashion by tiny straps encrusted with rhinestones. As tight fitting as it was, though, the dress probably was in no danger of slipping off Marilou's body. And body was the word that flashed across my mind as I was greeted with a smile and a peck on the cheek. My mouth went dry.

Marilou had obviously recovered her aplomb. Relaxed and utterly charming, she asked me about the campus tour. She even dared to make some references to one or two of those sites which had been the scene of our late-adolescent passion. The general tone was that of slight bemusement, and by the time Amanda drove up, I had relaxed and was actually enjoying the almost bantering nature of our conversation. There certainly were new facets to Marilou's personality. I could not remember her having these swings from moodiness to sparkling animation. But then, it had been a long time, and many things had added to the dimensions of our personalities. I'd been doing a bit of mood swinging myself, from dejection and apprehension to elation, then back to apprehension and embarrassment.

Amanda was obviously excited. As we got into the Continental, she was explaining why she was a little late.

"Henry didn't get to the hotel until after five. He was waiting to hear from Joe, the inimitable Joe!"

Marilou interrupted.

"Did Joe get any important information for us?"

"Henry was excited about something Joe told him, but he wouldn't tell me about it. He said I'd have to wait until we were all together. He did say that he'd had a busy day himself, getting information from the coroner that dealt with Tillie's death, and that he also had tracked down a maid that worked for the Wexlers at the time of her death. I don't know how many people he had getting information for him, though I suppose it couldn't be too many because Henry doesn't want it to get out that he's on the track of something. How was your day, Don?"

I made some noncommittal remarks about the tour, and then partly out of curiosity and partly just to keep the conversational ball rolling, I asked Marilou what she had done all day, since she wasn't on the tour.

"Oh, I drove up to my place in the mountains. It's less than an hour's drive up South Canyon. I do all my writing there, where it's quiet. Commuting to the campus is a bit of a bore some times, but then my particular job doesn't require that I keep rigid hours. I don't like to make the trip at night, so I often take a room at the Union when there's something going on here in the evening."

So this explained why she stayed at the Union Building for the reunion. So much for any ulterior motive involving former love, Donald Moffett. And it also cast a different slant on Marilou's career. She had mentioned early-on that she did writing for some magazine, but evidently this was not just a sideline. The elegant clothes, the appearance of affluence, and her general aura belied her being just a mousy librarian. I decided now was the time to get more details about her life.

"Just what is it you do at the University library?"

"Oh, didn't I tell you? I'm in charge of the rare-books division. I am responsible for acquisitions, seeing that the available funds are spent wisely, and also occasionally getting collectors or estates to make donations of valuable items. We've gotten some really fine things this way."

Amanda laughed.

"Marilou is a genius when it comes to conning some old codger out of his leather-bound first editions. I do believe they sometimes think they are involved in a barter deal—give my books to the library in exchange for Marilou Baxter's body. Then all they get is a reception where they are presented a parchment thanking them for their largess, something to hang on their wall you know, and a public kiss from Ms. Baxter. But she makes them feel that just that was worth it, that plus the big tax write-off they get, of course."

Marilou didn't seem to mind Amanda's appraisal of her skills. As a matter of fact, though I couldn't see her face from the back seat of the car where I was sitting, I felt that she was exhibiting a sort of smug satisfaction. This discussion of Marilou's career was terminated by our arrival at the hotel, and in another few minutes we were again seated in the Davis suite, drinks in hand.

"Oh, it's been a great day!" Hank Davis was obviously bursting with excitement. "I hardly know where to begin; I guess I'll just follow the day as it unfolded." He took a deep draught of his Coors.

"By the time I got to the office this morning, my secretary had gotten together all the notices and articles about Tillie's death. On the surface it looked pretty routine. Maid's night off, Tillie alone, goes to garage, starts up the car and in due time is asphyxiated, but oddly, no suicide note. One article purported to quote friends saying that she had been depressed recently. Her husband was quoted as saying that she had not been feeling well for some time. No more. But the coroner in charge was mentioned by name, so I got an appointment with him. He was a bit reluctant to talk at first, but it turned out that he doesn't like the Senator's stand on a number of things. When he got wind of the fact that I just might be trying to pin something on Wexler, he loosened up."

Amanda managed to get in one sentence while her husband had another go at his beer. "If anyone could loosen up a coroner, Henry could!"

"So what the coroner told me might be quite important. There was evidence of a high alcohol content in Tillie's blood, and there were also traces of barbiturate, probably an ordinary sleeping prescription, but not enough to cause death. It was assumed that she had been drinking because she was depressed and to give her courage to end it all, maybe taking the sedative just to be sure that her suicide would work. I asked him if the alcohol and the sedative could have caused Tillie to pass out, and after he checked his records, he indicated that would be a strong possibility. He said yes, it might be possible for someone to have then put her into the car, turned on the engine, and then split, if she'd passed out, that is."

This time Amanda got in only one word: "Who?"

"Who? The honorable Senator from Colorado, of course. Joe called me late this afternoon. He also had a busy day, very busy. First he had to track down the woman who was the Senator's personal secretary at the time of Tillie's death. She no longer works for the Senator, but she is in another legislator's office, so Joe found her through some directory or other of the employees of our law-makers. Joe would know how to get that sort of information!"

"As I told you last night, Joe has a real way with the ladies, and she agreed to have drinks with him after work. Well, it turns out that she has absolutely no love for the Honorable Senator from Colorado. Joe found out during the conversation that she was at one time having an affair with her boss and probably thought she might be the next Mrs. Wexler after she heard of

Tillie's death. When it became clear that that was not to be, she left his office in a huff and has borne him a grudge ever since. Joe says that she remembers the events of Tillie's death very clearly, as well she might."

It was Marilou who spoke this time, as Hank went to the bar for another Coors. It was with considerable venom in her voice that she said, "I can certainly understand how she felt. You might say that I bear him a grudge also, though not as much as you, Amanda."

Amanda was silent at this point, probably reliving some unpleasant episodes in her years with Bob. But Hank was back, and none of us had the opportunity for more personal comments.

"I guess I forgot to tell you that Joe had earlier checked the Senate roll call that morning, and Wexler indeed had been there for a vote taken around noon. BUT there was another vote late in the afternoon on some amendment or other to a pending bill. Joe thought it had been rather unexpected—some Legislator had gotten his pet project on the floor sooner than anyone had thought he could. Senator Wexler had not voted that time. Well, when Joe talked to the ex-secretary, she said she remembered well what had happened. Wexler had come in to his office right after lunch and had called his wife. He'd asked his secretary to put the call through, but she didn't hear any of the conversation since he closed himself in his inner office. But right after that, he had his secretary get him a round-trip ticket to New York City, with a return to Washington the next morning. She was pretty sure that he had talked to some travel agent before telling her to get the ticket, because he knew flight numbers and times of arrival and departures. He must have dialed that number himself or even more probably had gotten the information some time earlier. He told her that some emergency had come up, but it was odd, she said, because he didn't give her the name of the hotel in New York where he would be, which was most uncharacteristic. She had thought maybe he was going to spend the night with some woman in New York, which shows that even then she didn't have many illusions about her boss's sex life."

Amanda's sardonic comment was more a hiss than words.
"The son-of-a-bitch!"
Unperturbed, Hank continued.

"It was late the next morning when the phone call came in from Denver. The maid had found Tillie dead in the garage after she came to work and, finding no instructions from Mrs. Wexler, had looked in the garage to see if the car was gone. It then took some time to get the police and emergency people called, and with the two-hour time difference, it was after lunch before Wexler's office was called by the Denver police. The secretary didn't know how to contact her boss, of course, but she did know when he was to return from New York. Actually, he breezed in only a few minutes after the call from Colorado had come in. She said at first he seemed stunned and then went into hysterical carryings on—her exact words, according to Joe—though she wasn't convinced even then that they were genuine. Joe said that that was when she let it slip that she'd been having an affair with her boss and didn't think he much liked his wife back in Denver, so why all the big fuss?"

The time seemed right for me to say something, though my question could hardly be called profound.

"But I don't see what all this has to do with our suspicions of murder. Bob went to New York, not to Denver. Did he hire someone to get Tillie drunk and drug her and put her in her car?"

Hank shook his head a bit impatiently.

"I'm not finished! Wait till all the evidence is in. But of course, I'm at fault. I skipped to Joe's report too soon. By the middle of this afternoon, I had tracked down the maid that had been working for the Wexlers. Her name was in one of the news items about Tillie's suicide."

Amanda snorted, "Murder!"

"The woman works for some people we know, Amanda, the Howards. Remember how they were bragging on their cook the night we had dinner with them? Her name stuck in my mind, and on a guess I called the Howard residence, and sure enough, it was the same, one and only Chiquita. Remember, we kidded about the possibility of our having bananas for desert because of that silly old song, "Chiquita Banana?" I'd never have remembered it otherwise."

Amanda was agape. "I do remember all that. It seemed such an improbable name, even here in Colorado where we have so many Mexicans. And we did make a bit of silly talk about it. I remember hoping that the poor woman couldn't hear us from the kitchen."

Hank continued.

"Fortunately, the Howards weren't having a party tonight, so I dashed out to their place to talk to Chiquita, hoping Joe wouldn't call while I was gone. Since they still live in that big old house out in Park Hill, it didn't take me too much time. Chiquita is really very sharp, probably why she is such a good cook too. She could remember the events of the day Tillie died very clearly."

"Murdered," Amanda could again be heard muttering.

"Innocent until proven guilty, my dear," Hank replied, and then went on with his report.

"Chiquita had taken the call from Wexler to his wife late in the morning. That tied in with the secretary's saying it was right after lunch, considering the time difference. Chiquita said she didn't know what was said, but some time after Tillie had hung up, she came into the kitchen and asked Chiquita to fix something for dinner that could be heated in the microwave, and that it should be enough for two. She didn't say that her husband was coming home, however. It seems Chiquita didn't stay through dinner unless Wexler was home or there was a party."

"Would Tillie have been having someone in for dinner when her husband was gone?" Marilou inquired.

"I asked Chiquita that," Hank answered, "and she said that it wasn't particularly unusual. Mrs. Wexler had a lot of arty friends, she said, people her husband didn't particularly like, so she often saw them when he was out of town, had them over for a free meal and arty talk, Chiquita said. I don't think she liked Tillie's friends either."

Reunion With Murder

"So is the implication that one of her so-called friends did her in?" I was still being obtuse, but Hank didn't seem to mind.

"Of course, we probably will never know who shared the casserole Chiquita said she'd made for Tillie, and you're right, Don, on the surface it would seem that Wexler went to New York, not Denver. But, it would have been perfectly possible for him to get a direct flight to Denver from New York. Considering his possible plans, he wouldn't have had his secretary get those tickets. But he took the chance of getting the tickets himself as soon as he got to New York. I'm having old flight schedules checked to see if he could have done this, and there even may be some chance that we can get a record of his having purchased such tickets. Old records may still be available from either the airline or from American Express. His ex-secretary said he always used his American Express card—the gold one, of course. None of this common Visa or Master Card for the Senator from Colorado. We should know for sure by Monday. The two-hour time differential would definitely be to his advantage in this *modus operandi.*"

Now we all understood Hank's thinking. It was Marilou who verbalized it.

"Oh, I see now. You think Bob called his wife to tell her he would be home for dinner. He then had the secretary make the reservation to New York, and he left almost immediately. From New York he flew to Denver, getting there maybe at eight or nine o'clock in the evening. He would have rented a car—hey, there's another charge on his credit card if that is available—and drive home for late supper with Tillie. They have drinks, he slips the barbiturate into her drink. When she passes out, he puts her in her car, starts the motor, and then splits. Could there have been a night flight from Denver back to New York that he could have taken, so that he could get back to Washington by late morning?"

"That remains to be seen," Hank replied. "We're checking on that. It would be a tight schedule, so tight that no one would think of his doing such a thing. But even if we can prove that he flew to Denver that night, it still doesn't prove that he drugged Tillie's drinks. It would look bad, though. He'd have some explaining to do."

Amanda shook her head.

"If proving Wexler killed his wife is difficult, how about our suspicions that he engineered Jake's death?"

Hank shrugged his shoulders and turned the palms of his hands upward.

"That will be impossible, I fear."

Silence fell on the group, and Hank's elation over the information he had gotten seemed to be draining away about as fast as the water in a bath tub when the plug is pulled. This gave me opportunity to introduce the Senator's proposition.

"Bob bent my ear for some time during the brunch this morning. He wants me to join his campaign staff for the summer, under the impression that a political scientist can somehow help him to, as he put it, communicate with his electorate. I think what he means is that I would help him figure out how to con the voters into voting for him. He made it rather clear that I would not be a part of establishing policy. He said that my not being a resident of Colorado was an advantage, as I would be coming in with no preconceived notions on divisive matters. Little does he know what prejudices I'd be bringing to his campaign! And his naivety as to just what a political science prof. knows and doesn't know is monumental, at least in my own case. Teaching at DeMott University for nearly two decades has not prepared me for the realities of Colorado politics. I'm afraid that by the time I'd learned what I'd need to know, the campaign would long since be over, if Bob hadn't fired me before that."

As I talked, I realized that I seemed to be implying that I definitely had no intention of taking Bob up on his proposition. If indeed this were the case, it was the first I was aware of it. My ditherings up to this moment had been anything but definitive. The other three looked at me with various expressions of amazement on their faces. Since no one said anything, I had to continue, and my real indecision or lack of same began to show. I couldn't disguise my venality indefinitely.

"He made it sound very attractive. I'd be paid for several months of work what I earn in a year teaching. I'd have free use of an apartment in one of the high-rise buildings his wife's family owns and the possible use of a summer place in the mountains part of the time." I forbore mentioning that Bob had implied that Marilou might also be considered a fringe benefit. "I'd be working with his Denver staff and with him on weekends when he flies out from Washington. Actually, I could arrange to be away from my teaching the summer term very easily. There's a young man on the faculty who would be only too glad to take my classes."

"But do you think you could pull it off?" Hank's voice carried a message of real excitement. "You could well become privy to a lot of really valuable information, you know, working with him and his staff."

Amanda interrupted. "But if he found out that you were funneling information to us, it could be a bad scene. The honorable Senator might well accomplish what he failed to do twenty-six years ago on that snow bank!"

"Oh, Don, you couldn't take the risk!" Marilou sounded convincingly concerned.

Hank seemed unaware of the women's comments. After a moment he began to talk, almost as if to himself.

"That would give us a tremendous opportunity to find out just what is going on behind the scenes. What Wexler says in his speeches and news releases and what he actually believes or intends to do if reelected are entirely different things. His record during his first term was satisfactory on enough issues to give him some credence with the electorate. He managed to side-step some really controversial votes by not showing up for roll call. And he's a master of double talk, as we no doubt will have opportunity to hear tonight. It's felt that he considered his first term a sort of learning experience and an opportunity to make contacts and find out how to play the game. It's a second term that scares us. The environmentalists think maybe he is on their side, but there are rumors that the VonBronigan interests are covertly involved in the development of some mountain property they got control of through their mining operations. They want to build a big ski resort and hotel complex which would involve destroying a lot of fine timber and wild-life habitat. And water is at issue also. There is a stream on the property which is vital for fishing and for some foothill agriculture, but except in years of very heavy snows there is not enough water to support its present use plus a big development like that presumably envisioned by the VonBronigan Group. There is even some conjecture that the project is already under way, though no one can seem to get into the property to see for sure. The only road into it is posted with as many warnings as a nuclear testing site would have, with an armed guard very much in evidence. Presumably no legal permits have been granted for a project, but Wexler is no doubt by now in a position to know where pay-offs can be made to insure the necessary protection for the project."

Then, indicating that Hank had indeed heard the protests made by his wife and by Marilou, he added, "There would be danger involved, of course. There always is when one is garnering information that people don't want to get out. I've been in that situation any number of times. I'd not ask anyone to take the risk, but if one volunteers..."

Well, I hadn't felt that I had volunteered for anything. But Amanda's and Marilou's concern for my safety, instead of making me more cautious, frankly had the opposite effect. I've never considered myself to be the macho type, but with those two beautiful women expressing such concern for my well-being, I found myself figuratively flexing my muscles and beating my chest. And the charismatic Hank had obliquely implied that he thought I could pull it off. He had also made it clear that risking one's life was just part of the true American male's duty. If he could do it, why couldn't I? So I heard myself saying things that I hadn't really thought through.

"Well, I can be pretty discrete if needs be. And as long as Bob didn't know I was involved with you, I don't think I'd be in much danger. I'd be on the alert this time, now that we know what sort of a man we're dealing with...no more late afternoon slides or skiing lessons on glaciers with friend Bob." Then with real bravado, "I'm able to take care of myself, you know."

I almost looked around asking, "Who said that?" They might think that I could take care of myself, but I didn't have the slightest idea whether or not I could. Actually, I was pretty sure I couldn't, so why didn't I just say as much?

"Oh, but we shouldn't let you do it!" interjected Marilou. I suddenly realized that she was holding my hand. Amanda looked bemused. Then becoming very serious, she turned to her husband.

"Do you really think we should let Don put himself in such a position?"

There it was again. Somehow everyone seemed to feel I had bravely volunteered for this noble and dangerous assignment. Hell, venality and revenge had been the only motives that had me even remotely considering getting involved, and maybe sex. I tried to back-pedal.

"What worries me the most"—not my ability to defend myself against a murderer, of course—"is that I don't know whether *I* will be able to supply the Senator with the sort of information and guidance he wants."

Good God, there I was impugning my professional ability as a trained political scientist rather than lose any face as a macho male! Every time I opened my mouth, another ridiculous statement came out. So why not just shut up before it was too late? Except it probably was already too late. Anyway, when I did shut up, Hank or the lovely ladies just pushed me farther in the direction of what more and more seemed to me to be sure-fire disaster. All I needed was just one more little shove and I'd be done for. That little shove, damn it, of course came from Marilou.

"Oh, Don, you have become such a confident, with-it person! So self-assured!" Then turning to Amanda, she added, "Isn't it amazing how we change with the years?"

Just to be sure that the enlistment of Professor Donald Moffett as Secret Agent No. 1 in the vendetta against a double murderer was complete, Hank began to outline the *modus operandi*.

I swear I'd never said I'd do it. But there it was. Oh, well....

As Hank outlined what my role would be, I became more and more terrified, absolutely convinced that I couldn't pull it off. Adding to my distress was the fact that Marilou's hand was still over mine, and at one point I was sure she started to move her hand to my thigh but then thought better of it. Why didn't I pull my hand away? Why didn't I tell Hank to forget it—I was going back to the peaceful Midwest? Well, I firmly believe that each of us has a seed of selfdestruction lying dormant somewhere deep in that part of the brain that makes decisions. It is just waiting for some water and a little fertilizer to make it start to grow. Hank and Marilou had furnished both, especially lots of the latter. My seed was bursting forth into some wild and thorny shrub that shortly would have me hopelessly enmeshed in its tangle of spikey branches. There flashed before my mind the picture of a wild animal—I think it was a goat—in just such a situation, probably from some National Geographic T.V. special. Or was it from an old family illustrated Bible? Anyway, I was feeling like a trapped goat, a scapegoat about to be slaughtered, and the thorns were already scratching deeply!

Hank suddenly stopped laying out our strategies. Looking at his watch, he jumped up, reminding us that we had to get back to the Union Building for the banquet. Even as we stood up and prepared to leave the suite, Marilou's hand was holding my arm. She evidently was a woman turned on by a man of danger. No wonder it had been so easy for Bob to take her away from me twenty-six years ago! I was caution personified then, and had continued to be during the intervening years for that matter, until the last two days that is! Nor did things get any better during the drive back to the Union. Now there were four of us, so Marilou sat in back of the Continental with me. I sat in one corner, but Marilou sat very much in the center of the seat, a good portion of her body—THAT body—pressed up against mine. I had my hand in my lap, but her hand was on top of mine, not quietly resting there but sort of squeezing. Wiggling finger tips managed to make contact with my leg. I finally had enough sense to make the pretense of needing a handkerchief, so I got my hand free. Actually, I probably could have used a handkerchief to wipe my brow, though all I did was fake a discrete blowing of my nose and then took much time to clean my glasses. Marilou got the message, but I had the distinct impression that she in no way was giving up. Now about that fringe benefit to which Bob had alluded...?

CHAPTER 6

Hank dropped Amanda, Marilou, and me off in front of the Union Building before parking the Continental. As we were getting out of the car, he again stressed that I should not be seen consorting with the Davises. However, Amanda, Marilou, and I went through the lobby to the door leading into the ballroom where the banquet was to be held. It was late, and we could see that a lot of people were already seated at their tables. There were still a few people in the lobby, but some of them did not appear to be our old classmates. Amanda whispered that the press was on hand because of the Senator's speech.

Just as we entered the ballroom, a woman who seemed to have been given the task of seating arrangements rushed up to Amanda. I recognized her as having been a girl who always had been overly-eager to please, unsure of herself, and very nervous. Twenty-five years had not changed her a bit. If anything, she was more up-tight than ever.

"Oh, Amanda, I'm so glad you're here! I just didn't know what to do! Senator Wexler came to me just as people were starting to be seated, and he insisted, just really demanded, that Donald Moffett be seated at his table, next to his wife. And he said that Marilou Baxter should be seated next to Don. I just didn't know what to do. We'd decided, you know, that Hortense and her husband should be at the Senator's table because her husband is State Republican Chairman, and of course the University President and his wife and your co-chairman and her husband, the McFarlands, were to be there. You know I thought you and Henry should be at the Senator's table for the same reason, but you had already said you didn't want to be there with the Senator. And of course, then I remembered that you'd been married to him once. So now I decided that the only thing to do was to ask the McFarlands to take the place reserved for Donald Moffett, but it was a single, and I had to ask another lady whom I

Reunion With Murder

didn't recognize but seemed to be alone to take the place where we had Marilou sitting, so the McFarlands could be together, but it was so embarrassing because I didn't know her name, the lady I asked to move, I mean, and you weren't here, and oh, dear, I just didn't know how to handle it. I hope I did right, Amanda. The Senator is our guest of honor, and I just didn't know what to say, and…!" All this seemed to be on one breath, a truly remarkable performance.

Amanda took all this in stride, cool and collected.

"That's alright, dear. You handled it marvelously. I'm just so glad you didn't put the Davises at the head table."

Then turning to Marilou and me, she added, "You two run along and sit with the big shots. Make hay while the sun shines, Don, and you too, Marilou." This last was with a leer at Marilou, who had the grace to look embarrassed. None of this made any sense to the seating lady, of course, but she was already fluttering off, no doubt to cope with some other monumental crisis. I hoped she'd get her breath before having to again communicate with anyone. Just then Hank came through the door, so Marilou and I moved on quickly toward the table at the end of the room where Senator Wexler and his wife were still standing, greeting people who passed by.

As Marilou and I made our way down the long room, past the tables of eight, I had ample opportunity to observe Jessamin VonBronigan Wexler. Bob's telling me to anticipate the encounter was well-founded. She was absolutely stunning. She could have passed for twenty-one, at least from where we were at my first viewing—and I use that word advisedly. Wavy blonde hair fell to bare shoulders. There were no straps at all on this gown. The pale green embroidered material, studded with tiny pearls, seemed to have been plastered on to her body. I hadn't the slightest idea at first what held the gown on, but as we approached the table, it became clear to me that the task of keeping the dress from slipping to the floor had been delegated to her breasts. And a great job of discharging that duty they were doing! They were admirably endowed for the task at hand.

Oswald G. Ragatz

My expressive face must have given me away once again. I'd not realized that Marilou had been holding my arm as we had eased our way between the tables and other unseated late-comers who were looking for their place cards. But suddenly I could feel her hand stiffen, and then she dropped her arm to her side. I heard her whisper in my ear, "For God's sake, Don, stop drooling."

I had no time to be embarrassed, however, as we had nearly reached our goal, and Senator Robert Wexler boomed out, "Don and Marilou! Around here, by Jessamin and me."

As we rounded the table to the two empty seats, Bob continued. "Don Moffett, this is my beautiful wife, Jessamin. I've already told Jessamin all about how my oldest and dearest friend is going to come aboard our team of supporters as an expert in demography."

So if I had still had any ideas of extricating myself from this developing plot, I could forget them. Once again, fate, in the guise of old classmates, friends or foes, had intervened. By making the announcement public, Bob figured, and rightly so, that any indecision on my part would be taken care of. Out of the corner of my eye I saw a young man in a sport coat standing apart from the group at the head table, obviously frantically taking notes. The press, no doubt. But no time for such details.

I couldn't help but wonder if Bob Wexler knew the meaning of the term demography, and if he did, just how he expected me to apply my presumed knowledge of the subject to the benefit of his campaign.

Jessamin was shaking my hand, her almond-shaped green eyes gazing at me as though she had been introduced to Zeus, just down from Olympus for a night on the town with simple mortals. At close range, I could see that she was not twenty-one after all, *au contraire*. But whatever her age, it was well disguised by professionally applied cosmetics, ministered no doubt by experts in the maintenance of eternal youth for the rich and beautiful. Maybe even a face lift or a tuck here and there had helped. A diamond choker at Jessamin's neck possibly was

Reunion With Murder

meant to lessen the impact of the expanse of unblemished bare flesh that extended from her chin (no telltale sagging there!) to the top of her low-cut gown. However, this actually only called more attention to that phenomenon. It was obvious that this was one woman who had no intention of hiding her charms under the proverbial bushel, whatever that old saw means.

The diamonds around Jessamin's neck and those on her fingers and in the long dangling ear rings made the crystals of Marilou's dress look like discount-house imitations, which, of course, I suppose they had to be, even as elegant a dress as Marilou's actually was. But any discomfort Marilou might have been feeling in the presence of the glittering Jessamin was, at that moment, being tempered by the Senator's slightly too-long kiss followed by a torrent of palaver as to Marilou's appearance. Not that I would have disagreed with what he was saying had I not been under the spell of the radiant Mrs. Wexler.

As we were being seated, Jessamin was indulging in a bit of palaver herself. She'd heard SOOO much about me for SOOO long, Bob's VERY best friend for EVER and ever, and now that we had at LAST met, she could see IMMEDIATELY why Bob was SOOO fond of me.

She may have been a native of Colorado, but the accent was definitely East-coast Vassar or Wellesley. Bob had assumed the responsibility of holding Marilou's chair for seating—he had maneuvered so that he was sitting between the two women. Of course, I discharged the same duty for Jessamin, and as I did so, her slender fingers with their extra half-inch of scarlet nails slipped down my forearm seductively.

The memory of that meal will remain forever a total blur. I assume that the food was excellent. I do remember that there was a soup course, because I had great difficulty keeping my hand steady so as not to spill the soup on the table-cloth, on me, or worse still, on Jessamin. It was about that time that I became aware of the fact that I was underdressed, considering where I had been seated. All the other men at the head table were in dinner jackets. Of course, very few other men in the room had bothered to dress formally, and many of the women were not in long dresses. But this merely heightened the impact of Jessamin, and I should add, also of Marilou and of Amanda. The other two women at our table wore conservative, long, dark-colored dresses, which partially camouflaged their matronly figures.

I also remember that the *entrée* was fillet, because Jessamin commented that it was too bad the committee had chosen something so ordinary. Needless to say, I did not tell her that fillet was anything but ordinary in the Moffett household. She seemed to be a dreadful snob, but at the same time she made one feel that the snobbery was quite justified and acceptable, maybe even charming.

On my other side was the wife of the University President. She contributed almost nothing to the conversation and seemed to me to be totally bored except when she inquired worriedly as to her husband's state of health. Her husband kept looking at the elegant food as though he had been presented with a plate of uncooked tripe and a cup of hemlock. He kept popping Maalox tablets into his mouth when he thought no one was looking. I decided that this was probably one too many banquets to which he had been impelled to grace with his august personage during the commencement festivities of the preceding week. The others at the table were held in thrall by Senator Wexler, who was expounding on subjects ranging from life in Washington to various international and domestic crises being faced (bravely and wisely he implied) by our lawmakers. The noise in the room, the clatter of dishes, and the frequent glissandi and pluckings of a harpist who had been engaged to provide dinner music all made it difficult for me to pay much attention to the Senator. Anyway, it was much more rewarding to concentrate on Jessamin.

As the meal progressed, Jessamin's demeanor underwent a subtle change. Somewhere through the salad course, served after the main course (was that or was it not "western style"), I realized that she was no longer emitting the cliches, with every third word underlined, as she had at first. As a matter of fact,

Reunion With Murder

she had been asking me some pointed questions and had listened carefully to my replies. Where had I gotten my graduate degrees (Yale seemed to meet with her approval), what courses did I teach (she seemed to be satisfied), and what were the titles of my three major publications. When I said that my last book was titled, "The Demographics of Minorities in Selected Urban Areas: a Key to Understanding Certain Political Implications," instead of changing the subject to the weather or to the latest N.B.A. game, the usual reaction when one of my book titles was mentioned, Jessamin dropped all her artifices and began to ask some very penetrating questions. She listened with intensity and, I felt, with genuine understanding of what I was saying. Of course, I blossomed under this sort of attention.

By the end of desert, I had realized that this was no air-head bimbo nor even a self-centered socialite, contrary to first impressions. Just before the University President stood up to give his brief welcoming comments, I heard Jessamin say, "You are all that Bob said you were and more. You will do very nicely, if you can tolerate the shit you will have to put up with the next few months. We need you very badly, and..."

I was taken aback by the scatological term, but the conversation had to cease as the University President, between surreptitious burps, told us what a wonderful class we were, such a cause of pride to the University, etc. etc.

Then the State Chairman of the Republican Party hefted his considerable weight out of his chair and windily introduced the speaker of the evening. After a lengthy list of presumed noble characteristics attributed to the Honorable Senator Robert Henry Wexler—humanitarian, staunch adherent to the democratic process as envisioned by our noble forefathers, student of world politics, environmentalist, brother of all minorities, loyal friend, etc., etc. ad nauseam, I was thinking to myself, "cheat, womanizer, opportunist, murderer at least twice over," and then I glanced at Jessamin and saw those green eyes looking at me with the most penetrating gaze I hope never to be subjected to again. Had she read my mind, or had I actually said the words I had been thinking? But applause did not permit further perusal of this possibility.

I had the feeling that the applause was as much in appreciation of the fact that the introduction was over as it was in respect for old classmate, Bob Wexler. The press was moving from the lobby into the far end of the room, notebooks in hand. A few flash bulbs went off, and the harpist made a not very successful but valiant attempt at playing an old Colorado song—"C-O—L-O—R-A—D-O, I'm a mile high feelin' fine. I jus' got back from my mile-high shack in this healthy, wealthy, wonderful state of mine."

This was hardly the vehicle suitable for displaying a harpist's technique. I could tell she had never heard the silly tune because she was squinting at a music manuscript someone had shoved onto her music stand. For that matter, very few people in the room probably even remembered the song, if they ever had known it. I was particularly bemused by the implication that the Senator had just gotten back from his shack in the mountains. "I'll bet the VonBronigan mountain pad is some shack!" was probably written all over my mobile countenance. I glanced at Jessamin to see if she was reading my mind again, but her whole attention was directed at her husband. Nancy Reagan could have taken several lessons from Jessamin in projecting wifely adoration. I couldn't help but wonder if she really was that enamored of the old letch—excuse me, murderer. Maybe I should warn her. Oh, for heaven's sake! I was discovering an alarming potential for being suckered by beautiful women, buried somewhere in my id, wherever that is. I thought I'd conquered any weakness in that direction twenty-four years ago when I bade Marilou farewell and put her on that bus for Boston. But now this unwelcome weakness of character seemed to be seeping out like some virulent toxic waste, mucking up my life at every turn. Maybe the E.P.A. could be called into help me...the Senator had just mentioned E.P.A.

I forced myself to concentrate on the Senator's remarks. After all, if I were to be one of his chief advisors (My God!), I'd

Reunion With Murder

better find out what was going on. For the next half hour, I tried valiantly to figure out what Bob was saying—and what he was not saying. It really sounded on the surface as though he were making remarks of great import. At first, the reporters at the far end of the room frantically took notes, but after a bit, along with me and probably anyone else in the room trying to make sense out of the speech, they gave up. A couple of the reporters were obviously slack-jawed. One quietly slipped out. I thought the University President was going to be ill; he was actually a greenish color, and more Maalox tablets were being slipped into his mouth. The State Chairman of the Republican Party wore a beatific smile, and not a facial muscle moved for the whole half hour that the Senator waxed eloquently, if pointlessly. Jessamin adored, the other two wives looked bored, and Marilou exuded an air of unyielding grimness.

As I tried to listen, an editorial by a noted columnist—I think it was R. Emmett Tyrrell—came to my mind. He was writing about some legislation or other that Congress was fighting over. It went something like this: "The tortured meanings that politicians force on such terms as 'quotas,' 'affirmative action,' 'racial goals,'...and other arcana are concocted to dissuade ordinary Americans from any further consideration of these dread topics." That isn't an exact quote, but it will do. I remembered the editorial partly because the word arcana had not been in my usual vocabulary before...a great word! As I recall, Mr. Tyrrell went on to point out how politicians disguise such things as tax increases by calling them revenue enhancements, or by calling welfare checks entitlements. This is just the beginning of their manipulation of words, creating miasma and obfuscation of truth.

Well, Senator Wexler had all the politicians' bull down pat. He dished out the words with such charm, such enthusiasm, such sincerity that it seemed that they certainly must mean something, if only the listener weren't so stupid. Part of the time I was almost convinced myself, and I know I'm no dummy...no great brain but no dummy. It should have been patently apparent to all that he wasn't saying anything, since in a half hour he touched on every controversial topic faced by our country—everything from race to environment to armament to abortion to peace to Colorado water problems to inflation to the national deficit to Colorado finances to oil and mining rights to pollution to the destruction of the ozone layer to toxic waste to our noble soldiers back from the Middle East to the P.L.O.-Israeli conflict, and on and on. He seemed always on the right side until you thought twice about what he had said, and then you realized that he wasn't on any side at all because he had taken no stand. He had listed the nation's problems but had not presented any solutions. But somehow the less perceptive would go away thinking that Senator Wexler agreed one-hundred percent with them on each and every one of the issues. The worst part of it, they would vote for him. But such charm! No wonder the women fell for his line.

Then the speech was over. Considerable applause acknowledged yet another success in the political maneuverings of Senator Wexler. No longer did Jessamin need to assume the adoring stance, and as she turned her eyes to me, I was sure I saw a cynical sneer. It was just a brief moment, and then she was all adoring smiles again. Flash bulbs blinded us, the University President emitted a surreptitious burp into his handkerchief, and Marilou was so angry that she seemed in danger of having a stroke. I couldn't help but wonder what Amanda and Hank thought of it, but I knew I'd find out soon enough.

Mrs. McFarland, from the seat originally reserved for me, was tapping on her water glass to get the attention of the noisy room. Having thanked the Senator, the University President, all the committee members who had worked to make the reunion the rousing success that it had been, she finally remembered to thank co-chairperson Amanda Davis for all of her wonderful ideas.

Her latter remarks were made nearly inaudible because of the confusion involved with the arrival of the same dance band that had played the evening before for the buffet. Since a small portion of the floor was to be used for dancing, waiters were shoving tables together, thereby inconveniencing the people still seated. Mrs. McFarland's final remarks were completely lost. Had she offered a benediction, a malediction, or just told us to go to hell? No one would ever know, possibly not even her husband, who sat next to her in the other commandeered seat.

By now there was no longer any opportunity for meaningful conversation at the head table. People were coming up to shake the Senator's hand. The State Republican Chairman and wife, Hortense, were in full cry doing what it is that politicians do best—pump hands, slap backs, kiss cheeks, and utter inanities. The University President, handkerchief in hand over his mouth, was led away by his worried wife, and Marilou stood forlornly. As I was about to rescue Marilou, though the Wexlers were between us, Jessamin turned her attention away from her husband. Those green eyes were looking into me—not AT me, INTO me—with a frightening intensity. In a voice so low only I could hear, she said, "Now you see what your job is. They'll wake up tomorrow morning and begin to wonder what he said. It will be up to you to find out which segment of the population will figure out that he doesn't say anything, and if they constitute enough votes, you'll get him in focus so they will think they know what he said. Finding out which voters are important to us is your job. But we'll talk later. Now you ask your Ms. Baxter to dance. She looks bereft. But I want a dance with you a little later."

This last was not in the nature of an invitation. It was an order. It was becoming clear who would be calling the plays in this new venture of mine. Maybe it wasn't that pair of lovely boobs holding up that dress Jessamin wore after all. It more likely was a steel backbone. Now I understood why Bob Wexler had insisted I sit at the head table by Jessamin. As usual, he was successful at getting someone else to do his work for him. But in this case, I wasn't at all sure that Jessamin was the patsy. I doubted very much that Bob would be able to cast her off—or murder her—when and if she was no longer of use to him. It might well be the other way around. I found myself being very pleased with the prospect of someone casting off Bob Wexler—maybe even murdering him? I moved over to Marilou Baxter, and in a few moments we were again on the dance floor, moving as one to the strains of yet another golden oldie that took us back two-and-a-half decades.

For a bit, nothing was said. Then Marilou asked me what I thought of Bob's speech. A few pithy replies seemed to reassure her that we agreed. After we had done a couple of spins and a dip, I broke the silence.

"I glanced at you a couple of times while Bob was talking, and you looked furious. How come? Bored maybe, but why so furious?"

"Oh, I was. It's sort of hard to explain. Of course, I have this long-standing, basic anger to start with. Then he made remarks to me at the brunch this morning and again all through dinner—little personal asides—that I resented. And now all this pretense of being such a great, upstanding savior of mankind on top of what we suspect him of, it was just too much."

The business about personal remarks was too much for me not to follow up, so I stuck my neck out, way out.

"Yea, I saw him stop by your table at the brunch, and you looked mad then, too. So what's he up to? Trying to get you in the sack again?"

The instant I said that, I knew I'd probably gone too far. My own old resentment was showing, and I hadn't intended to slip. But oddly enough, Marilou didn't seem to resent the crack. There was no stiffening of her body, indicative of resentment. After a moment, during which we negotiated rather gracefully a couple of old dance steps, she answered.

"It's not his sack he wants me in, but it seems he is determined to get me into yours—or you in mine, whichever way you look at it. At brunch I just figured it was a crude remark, but after tonight I think I have it figured out. He still isn't sure you are going to join his staff, in spite of his pronouncement in front of everyone. And in his typical way of using people in any way he can to further his goals, he figures I could be an added incentive for your sticking around for the summer, a sort of sex bait. It was all pretty degrading!"

A dip and a spin and Marilou was back in my arms, as I replied.

"He made some similar comments to me, actually. I believe he referred to you as a fringe benefit."

Marilou missed a step at that one.

"Fringe benefit?! Not even a major enticement? That bastard!"

In a tone of voice I hoped would sound teasing, I replied, "So you considered it a bum assignment? But it would all be in the name of the good cause of exterminating the good Senator. And maybe I could be considered a fringe benefit myself."

I should never, ever try to be funny or to engage in banter. I just end up in trouble. Marilou was trouble.

"I'd consider it a very enticing assignment, but not from Bob Wexler. I much prefer taking the responsibility of whom I sleep with myself, and for reasons other than revenge or of ridding mankind of a malevolent snake."

Then after a moment, she added, "I believe I made it very clear last night where I stand on the subject of your sharing my bed. And I might add, you made it clear where you stand—or possibly I could say, stood?"

This last was said with a tinge of hope, more like a question expecting a positive answer. I realized that in light of how tightly I was holding her, she might well have thought I had undergone a change of heart. As a matter of fact, at that moment, I wasn't at all sure that indeed I hadn't changed my mind about spending a night in the arms of this very attractive lady, this long-lost love of my youth. I really don't know what I'd have said next if there hadn't been a tap on my shoulder.

It was Bob Wexler, arm around the incredibly small waist of Jessamin.

Oswald G. Ragatz

"I've been dying to have a dance with the lovely Marilou, and Jessamin, judging from the look in those sparkling green eyes, would like to experience your legendary dancing prowess."

That was the first I'd heard about being a legend in my own time, on the dance floor or anywhere else, but then Marilou and I had been, as we would have said in the olden days of our youth, cutting a rug.

I wondered for a moment if Marilou would refuse, but refusing Bob Wexler anything took preparation, the bolstering of one's courage and the girding of one's loins. He was a master at catching one off guard and vulnerable. So in a moment, Marilou was being swept off across the floor in the Senator's arms, and I found myself tentatively putting my arm around that fabulous, lithe body of Jessamin. Did I feel a steel backbone? I wondered. I just hoped that nothing I would do would dislodge that dress from its tenuous moorings on her breasts.

But Jessamin, while a good enough dancer, was not interested in my promised expertise on the dance floor. Dancing was merely a pretext for continuing conversation that had not been completed during dinner. Well, directives—even orders—would be more appropriate. There was very little conversation as such.

"There will be a meeting at our home tomorrow afternoon at four o'clock. Bob's campaign manager, Ron Dawson, and my father and my uncle Karl will be there. They want to give you specific instructions on what is needed at this point. You'll be working with them more than with Bob, since he will be in Washington much of the time. I personally don't think they really know what they want. They're scared, because the polls indicate that Bob's opponent just may win the election. We have to come up with something new to capture needed support. And between you and me, we also have to be careful that the opposition doesn't come up with something that will smear the Wexler name. They are trying very hard. We know that there are people on the Denver Post, for example, that would like to see Bob hang, not the least of which is Henry Davis, who as you no doubt know is married to Bob's ex-wife Amanda."

We negotiated a couple of simpler dance maneuvers without misadventure.

"We are sure that there is a segment of the intelligentsia which is opposed to Bob but might be impressed by anything a professional such as you comes up with. That would help. But there are also minority groups with a sizeable voting power, usually going Democratic, which might swing to us if they can be convinced that Senator Wexler is for the little man, for the minorities, for the things that keep them with cash in their pockets. This is where you will be the most important, if I understand what your book was about. I'll be ordering it Monday. Who is the publisher?"

This was the first chance I had had to say a word. And that is just all it was, one word, my publisher's name, not even the "and Sons."

"I'm sorry you can't move into your duplex tomorrow, but since tomorrow's Sunday, you'll have to wait until Monday afternoon. It's in a high-rise we own, a mile or so off Capitol Hill on downtown. But you know Denver, don't you, from college days?"

I managed an "Oh, yes." But I didn't get a chance to add that Denver seemed to have changed much since I was last in Colorado, judging from the maps I had picked up at the airport.

"You rented a car, of course, to come up here. Just charge it to us. We'll give you the necessary charge cards for your expenses tomorrow, when you come out to the house. It takes a good fifty minutes to drive out to our place from downtown Denver. I'll give you the address when we finish the dance. I have a card in my bag."

Then the band stopped, and a moment later Bob and Marilou approached. Bob was exuding his customary charm.

"Thank you, Don, for letting me dance with this lovely lady. She is still the great dancer she used to be."

The idea that Marilou was somehow mine to be permitted to dance with someone of my choosing was bizarre. Then Bob was telling Marilou what a pleasant experience it had been. Looking at me again, he added, "I presume Jessamin has told you about the meeting at our place tomorrow afternoon. You will be there, won't you?"

This was the first time I'd been given a choice in any matter. I did manage to qualify my answer.

"Well, I haven't had time to change my plane reservations or call my wife to tell her of any change of plans."

"Wives and airlines mustn't presume to stand in the way of progress. You can, I am sure, explain to your wife about careers and politics." Bob's remark was met with notable stony silence on the part of the two listening women.

Jessamin handed me her address card as she and her husband moved on into the crowded dance floor. Marilou and I both understood that it was time to terminate our participation in the festivities. We saw Amanda and Hank leaving through the door to the lobby. Marilou muttered under her breath, "What a son-of-a-bitch he is!"

The Davises were standing just outside the door to the ballroom. As we passed them, Hank said quietly to me,

"Don, I'll be back and will come up to your room in a quarter of an hour. We need to talk." Then he and Amanda moved on out of the lobby, presumably going to their car.

Hank's announced return precluded any further opportunity for conversation of a personal nature between Marilou and me. I was greatly relieved, as I felt that things had for a moment gotten completely out of hand back there on the dance floor. For once I was grateful to Bob Wexler for having taken Marilou away from me. Well, not away from me, exactly—for asking Marilou to dance. Marilou and I took the elevator to our floor, and at her door I thanked her for her pleasant company, bade her a good night, and said I wanted to call my wife before Hank returned. She gave me a chaste peck on the check and in a moment was gone.

I went on to my room, and after a brief visit to the bathroom, I put in a call to Lucille at her mother's new number in Columbus. At that point, Columbus, Ohio, seemed light years away, and I was shocked to find that I was having to concentrate to bring the mental picture of Lucille, my wife of twenty-three years, into focus.

Oswald G. Ragatz

CHAPTER 7

It took only about a minute of conversation with Lucille to bring me back into the real world. She talked at some length about the problems of getting her mother settled, especially since it was over a week-end when service people weren't available. It had become apparent that Lucille was going to be needed in Columbus for all the next week, so when I broached the possibility (to put it mildly) that I wouldn't be returning home immediately, there was no adverse reaction. However, as I began to get into the matter of my being a technical advisor for Senator Wexler's campaign, there was a moment of reticence. But then Lucille warmed up to the idea, especially when I told her how much money would be involved.

Next I heard myself telling her about the duplex in the high-rise, and I was suggesting that as soon as she was finished in Columbus maybe she could come on out to Denver. So much for Bob's innuendos as to the potential of a liaison between Marilou and me. My guardian angel, champion of fidelity and honor, had won out yet again. Or as Bob Wexler would have put it, too bad I had to be such a Puritan.

But I wasn't going to be able to shift the responsibility of moral decisions to some mythical guardian angel that easily. Lucille reminded me that she was teaching summer term, and unlike my situation, there was no one else in the department who could take over her work. She pointed out to me that there were several students depending on completing her advanced sculpture course during the summer term so that they could get their B.F.A. degrees in August. Was I pleased or apprehensive? Maybe a bit of both. But any decisions regarding Marilou were definitely back in my court.

I did not tell Lucille anything about the sub-plot, namely proving that my employer, Senator Wexler, was a murderer. It was just too complicated, it involved Marilou—something I didn't particularly want to get into—and the situation was just too bizarre to try to explain over the phone. Anyway, Lucille would worry about me. Well, actually, I just didn't want to get into it. Lucille wasn't really a worrier.

We had talked about fifteen minutes when there was a tap on the door. I asked Lucille to hold on a minute while I let Hank in. Returning to the phone, I explained that one of the editors of the Denver Post had just arrived and that I had to sign off. I told her I loved her, and she replied that she loved me too. And then, in that same tone of voice she had used in the kitchen weeks before, she added, "Tell Marilou hello for me and that I said she should take good care of you."

Now what in the hell did she mean by that? In view of what George Bush Sr. might have called "the Marilou thing" of the past two days, it was little wonder that I had a sudden wave of guilt sweep over me. But how could Lucille have known? Women! My God, they seem to have these extra senses, sixth, seventh, umteenth. Marilou, Amanda, Jessamin, and now Lucille! I felt overwhelmed. It was with considerable relief that I turned to Hank, who had seated himself on the one chair in the room. I was ready for a man-to-man conversation, no women present to murmur "Murder", no big blue eyes—or green eyes—probing my soul or my id, stirring up the old libido, and no companion of two-decades-plus who seemingly could read me like a book. No, not like a book, like a printout faxed directly to Columbus, Ohio, a detailed study in depth of the current Donald Moffett.

"Your wife?" Hank's voice was all blandness. And as I nodded, he added, "But of course, you'd not be telling anyone else you loved her in that tone of voice." But the last sentence was delivered like a question, not like a statement of fact.

I felt like jumping up on the bed and yelling, "Will everyone please just get off my back!?" But of course I did no such thing. I just sat down on the bed and waited for Hank to get down to business. I kept thinking, "If I am so transparent, how can I presume to act as a double agent in a murder case?" But it wasn't I who was presuming. It was everyone else presuming! Just as there were those who presumed I could get Senator Wexler reelected.

I felt that Hank possibly was harboring similar thoughts as to my inability to carry out any subterfuges. He sat looking at me for a while, saying nothing. The silence was intolerable, so finally I apologized for not having anything to offer him to drink. The University Union did not include mini bars in their rooms.

"No problem," Hank replied. "I just need to get the next few days in perspective, but first I want to know what you thought of Wexler's speech."

Now that was something I could talk about! I minced no words in expressing my opinions. As I became more and more vehement in my comments, Hank looked more and more pleased. I finally ended by using an old cliché Lucille and I had read somewhere years ago, but it greatly amused Hank so he must not have heard it before. "Trying to grasp what the Senator says and make sense out of it is like gift-wrapping a chunk of Jell-o."

Hank finally quit laughing. "It IS amazing how Wexler can spout so many words that mean so little. But of course, that's his genius, his strategy if you will. Actually, his speeches are mostly written by hack writers he employs, but he tells them what he doesn't want said, and they're clever enough to come up with gems like we heard tonight. One of my colleagues at the Post suggested that they must have a big chart of clichés, and another big chart of issues. One writer throws a dart at ISSUES, another throws a dart at CLICHÉ'S, and thus the first sentence is born. And on and on, *ad nauseam*. I had hoped you'd feel the way you do, but I'm glad to hear you express it so, so definitely."

Then I told Hank about the various conversational bits I'd had with Jessamin. I concluded by saying that as far as I could see, I had no control at all over my destiny at this point Wexler—and Jessamin—had decided I was working for them, and that was that. Somewhat ruefully, I also added that I seemed to have been equally boxed into a corner where I was having to become a reluctant double spy. I half expected Hank to make some conciliatory noises and maybe say that if I didn't want to go through with all this, it was O.K. But no such luck. All he said was, "Fate does take over at times."

At that point I knew I had had it. There was no chance of my backing out. I'd been pusillanimous some time earlier and as a result had missed any chance for escape. In all honesty, I couldn't precisely remember just when I had been pusillanimous, but there must have been SOME time when I could have avoided all this mess. At any rate, there didn't seem to be anything to do now but forge ahead, so I stopped whining and asked a question.

"Am I right in thinking that Jessamin is the power back of the Senator's political career? As the evening wore on, I got the distinct impression that she is a steel hand in a velvet glove." As I said that, I realized what a dumb cliché that was, in view of that revealing gown she had worn, except that the dress did fit like the proverbial glove, I guess.

"Oh, at this point Jessamin is definitely the power behind Wexler," Hank answered. "In the first place, she probably married him just to give her and her family the prestige and the Washington connections they needed. Wexler needs the VonBronigan money to maintain the life-style to which he has become accustomed. And of course, he loves to be seen with a beautiful woman on his arm. Poor Tillie never fulfilled that particular need. It is a symbiotic relationship and as such is a fairly stable one. At this point, they both need each other. Now if Wexler doesn't get reelected, Jessamin might just decide he is excess baggage. It is doubtful that Wexler could find another woman who would offer him the advantages that Jessamin does, so he's not apt to be considering disposing of her, one way or another."

"How about his fooling around with other women?" I said. "That seems to have been his pattern in the past...once a letch always a letch. Would Jessamin decide she had enough of that and decide to dump him?" I remembered that brief look on her face after his speech. Hank's cynical laugh was revealing.

"I doubt very much if Jessamin Wexler would be in a position to make anything of Bob Wexler's amorous adventures. She is notorious for her own affairs. In some circles she is referred to as Platte River Pussy. She has become more discrete since getting involved with Washington society and becoming visible in the political scene, but I dare say she will be putting the fix on you before the week is up."

I thought Hank was going to give me some advice as to the inadvisability of succumbing to the green-eyed charms of Jessamin. But he paid me the compliment of assuming that I had enough sense to avoid that pitfall. I don't know that I had the same confidence in myself at that moment, however. I couldn't forget my shaking hand as I tried to get the soup spoon to my mouth at dinner.

I next explained about the summons to the Wexler home the next afternoon and about the duplex that I presumably was expected to occupy Monday afternoon. Hank rubbed his hands together in gleeful expectation.

"Oh, this is too good to be true! I knew nothing specific would come out of this speech tonight, contrary to Amanda's expectations. It was obviously just going to be another of those pompous nothings. However, I do think he may have lost the support of some of the more thinking listeners who could discern what a fraud he is by what he didn't say, by his lack of focus on anything. Unfortunately, there aren't enough voters around that are that perceptive. But having you appear from nowhere and almost immediately be in the Senator's inner circle is an unbelievable stroke of luck. I do believe that Amanda has a flair for intuitive deductions and the genius to put them into action, without her knowing why it is she does certain things. I don't have too much hope of our being able to pin a murder rap on Wexler, but maybe with the help of Joe, something will come of that after all. But I can't believe that you won't discover some nefarious plan that will enable us to derail the campaign, possibly something the VonBronigans are up to. Of course, if we can prove that Wexler murdered his second wife, or your friend Jake for that matter, so much the better. But as I said, I can't see our pulling that off. But first things first."

I stood up and went to the window. I had a wonderful view of part of the campus. In spite of the late hour, there were still people—couples, singles, and an occasional group—moving to their various destinations. The campus was well lighted, probably in deference to concerns about unwarranted attacks of one sort or another. That was something we hadn't thought much about twenty-five years ago. But maybe we should have been more cautious—suspicious. Jake would probably have been here at this reunion had he been more wary of the ulterior motives of friend Bob Wexler. And I wouldn't be here talking to Hank, and... Turning to Hank, I put an end to my musings.

"So what specifically do we do next? Please don't leave too much decision making up to me. I'm new at this cloak and dagger business. Teach the raw recruit the ABCs of the game."

"Well, tomorrow is Sunday, so there isn't much we can do."

Hank seemed to be thinking aloud. "Drive back to Denver in the morning, and get yourself a room at a suitable hotel for tomorrow night. I'd suggest one of the Embassy Suites. Keep your car, of course. You'll need transportation."

I interrupted to tell Hank that Jessamin said they would pick up the tab for the car. Nodding approval, Hank continued.

"Fine, let them do it. Amanda and I will be going back home tomorrow morning also. We'd love to have you stay with us, but that would be too dangerous. We must avoid any contacts that would tie you with me, or the Denver Post. As soon as you get your apartment and have a phone, call my office and leave your number with my secretary. Here's my office number. I'll put my home number on the back."

Hank took a card out of his coat pocket and wrote a phone number on the back before continuing.

"Do you think you remember the way up to that glacier on Jones Peak? I'd like to see that infamous setting, just out of curiosity."

After thinking for a few moments, I shook my head.

"I'm sorry, but I haven't the slightest idea how we got there. Bob was driving, of course, but I didn't know the mountains all that well, not being a native. Growing up in Kansas doesn't prepare one for the Colorado experience. We went up on a main highway quite a ways, then turned off on a small side road, and finally went on what I remember as being just two ruts through a sort of open pasture-like slope and then into some scrubby trees. But that was a long time ago. It may be a throughway now. I do remember that there was a spectacular view of the Front Range. Jones Peak itself, what we could see of it, wasn't all that notable."

"Well, never mind," Hank replied. "I'll get a map that shows the lesser peaks in the state, and we can find it. You wouldn't mind going with me up there, would you?"

I was sure that this was the first time I'd been asked if I minded doing anything. Not that I thought a negative answer would have been accepted. But just to be asked was a new experience in dealing with these strong-minded Westerners. And of course, I had no intention of saying no, not that Hank was waiting for an answer.

"We'll try to get that in sometime this next week after you find out what sort of a schedule you will be expected to follow. I don't know how we will arrange to get together—probably meet at some inconspicuous restaurant or bar down near my office. As to what you do for now, it's quite simple. Approach the whole thing as a professional job. You're hired to deal with demographics as applied to a senatorial campaign. I'm sure you'll need to do research on the Colorado voting patterns. You will be talking to people dealing with the campaign. Act as though your whole goal in life is to see Bob Wexler reelected to the Senate. But keep your eyes and ears open. And don't write anything down. Just remember, that's all, just remember. When we make contact, tell me what you have learned that may further our counter campaign. And do try to maintain a straight face. You do reveal your thoughts sometimes by your facial expressions, you know.

"Yes, I do know." I drily replied. "That has gotten me in trouble a number of times, especially with my wife."

Hank's laugh indicated that he didn't take this weakness of his newly-anointed spy too seriously. He stood up, and shaking my hand, added, "You may find this new game of cat and mouse a lot of fun. I have rather enjoyed this sort of thing over the years myself. Some day I'll have to tell you about some of the adventures Joe and I had in our muck-raking days in Washington. When I retire, I'm going to write a book. Well, thanks for your time. Leave your phone number with my secretary, and then I'll be in touch. Call me if anything comes up before Monday evening. Good night."

And as I closed the door after Hank's departure, I said to myself, "And if I live through this, I'm going to ask Hank if Joe has a last name."

CHAPTER 8

After Hank left, I went over to the window again and looked down on the campus, dark except for the pools of light under the ornamental street lights placed along the walks leading from building to building. The fifteen minutes of reality I had experienced while talking to Lucille had been displaced by a swirl of mental confusion. I was reminded of those shots one occasionally sees in nature films on television when the camera was slowed down to take a sequence of time exposures of the sky. When the film is then played back at normal speed, the clouds rush across the sky at great speed, creating menacing turbulence.

But after standing at the window for quite some time, oblivious to the movement of people on the walks below, the confusion in my mind began to dissipate. I was at last able to think more rationally and to adopt the sort of mental organization I urge my students to employ when beginning work on a difficult topic for a term paper or dissertation—use simple questions and give straight forward answers, and then the big picture will emerge. So I began a dialogue with myself that went something like this.

Question: Am I really so trapped by circumstances that I can not back out of the situation?

Answer: Of course not. These people who one way or another have been moving me about like a chess piece have no legal or moral control over me.

Question: Then am I actually expecting to be at the Wexler's at four o'clock tomorrow afternoon?

Answer: Well, yes.

Question: You are going on your own volition, on your own free will?

Answer: Certainly.

Question: Then does this mean that you intend to use your professional training to the best of your ability to do the job expected of you by Wexler and company?

Answer: Well, yes. My self-respect would not let me do otherwise. I'm a trained political scientist.

Question: So this means that you are committed to doing everything in your power to persuade the Colorado electorate to vote for that sleeze-bag murderer, Robert Wexler?

Answer: Well, yes and no. I mean, I'll do my best, but I am assuming that he won't be elected.

Question: So you don't think you are a good enough political scientist to do the job Wexler is hiring you to do?

Answer: Oh, no, it's not that.

Question: Then what the hell do you mean?

The clouds thickened, sped up, and again rushed across that mental T.V. screen of my mind. I waited, watching a couple on the walk below engage in some passionate kissing and groping. This slight diversion calmed down the fast forward to a reasonable pace again. Time for more questions.

Question: You have implied that professional integrity is important to you, and you have confidence in your abilities, so isn't there a sort of dichotomy here? Explain yourself.

Answer: (after some thought) It's a matter of determining the real goal.

Question: Oh? And what is the real goal? At the moment it seems as though the goal has been spelled out quite clearly by Senator Wexler, or more specifically, by his wife Jessamin.

Answer: No, No, No! The goal is proving that Bob Wexler was—is—a murderer. The assignment to work for him is just a means to put me into a position to obtain inside information about him, maybe finding something that will trip him up.

Question: Ah, now we are getting somewhere. So you believe that the end justifies the means?

Answer: Well, I suppose so, at least when one is attempting to prove murder.

Question: But you will be committing perjury every day you are working with and for the Wexler campaign. How does that fit in with your concept of honesty?

Answer: I'll have to work on that—keep the goal clearly in mind and assume that something will develop that will derail the campaign. I might even come across some facts other than murder which, if made public, would put the Senator out of the running.

Question: So now you would be in the same situation as the "plumbers" in the Watergate scandal, yes? Or perhaps more specifically, like those responsible for the dirty tricks played on McGovern during the Nixon-McGovern campaign. Do you think your behavior will be any better than that?

Answer: I don't know, I don't know! Get off my back!

Question: Ha! Just how do I do that? Your back is your back is your back as Gertrude Stein might have said.

Much pacing about the room followed. On the third time I passed the window, I noted that the amorous couple had disappeared, probably to some place more suitable for a seduction.

Question: Well, what's happened to that clear-thinking, steel-trap mind of yours? I've had no answer to my last question.

Answer: OK. OK! So I'm no better than a "plumber"! I'm a double agent! But my real loyalty is to Hank Davis, and the real goal is to unmask a murderer. It has nothing to do with politics, really. Colorado politics mean nothing to me, other than in the abstract.

Alter ego—no question, just a directive: That will have to do for now. Go take a shower and go to bed. Oh, yes, and make the shower a cold one. For the moment you seem to have forgotten that Marilou is just down the hall, probably lying in her lonesome bed hoping to hear a rap on her door.

Answer: Damn you! Damn you to hell!

The shower was long and cold, and my bed was lonesome also. But after a half hour of tossing and turning and mulling over the events and conversations of the past two days, I fell into a welcome sleep.

My watch showed eight o'clock when I was awakened by the ringing of the phone. I nearly knocked the phone off the night stand as I groped sleepily to answer it. Marilou's voice, all bubbling with vitality and charm, brought me wide awake.

"I hope I didn't call you too early. I just told the Davises good-bye, and I'm about to leave for my place up the canyon. We just had a cup of coffee in the cafeteria, but by the time I get home, I'll be ravenous. I may put together a Sunday morning brunch and eat it out on my deck, which incidentally gives one a marvelous view of the Front Range. The weather is perfect this morning. Hank said you had an appointment at four this afternoon, so I thought maybe you'd like to join me for a Baxter brunch—just to fill up the day. You wouldn't have to leave for Denver until two o'clock."

I realized that my self-induced conversation with myself the night before had not touched on this subplot of Marilou Baxter. So I lunged ahead. This invitation required a snap decision, although my mouth seemed to be functioning ahead of my rational thinking. I realized that I should do something about my errant mouth...

"Well, I had wondered what I'd do with myself until my four o'clock appointment. It's at the Wexlers, you know."

"Yes, I know," Marilou answered, with some acidity in her voice. "You will no doubt be introduced to The Group. My brunch would help prepare you for the ordeal. I understand that Jessamin likes to entertain at home by her pool, clad in the briefest of bikini and bra, so as to show off all the VonBronigan charms. Oops, I just can't think of her as a Wexler, somehow."

My mouth continued to emit words.

"Well, how would we work it? I mean, I'd need my car to go down to Denver, so I can't go with you in your car." (Oh, that was a deep, a very deep observation! Mouth, you are remarkable!)

"Oh, that's no problem," Marilou answered Mouth. "Meet me in the lobby as soon as you get dressed, and then we'll get our cars out of the parking lot and you can follow me. It's about three-quarters of an hour's drive up the canyon."

I am afraid my reply sounded less than enthusiastic. My mind was beginning to catch up with Mouth. "Give me twenty minutes. It, it sounds like fun."

"Oh, it will be. I guarantee! Money back, including postage." Marilou hung up, leaving me slightly appalled at what I had just agreed to do.

I staggered to the bathroom and looked in the mirror. Circles under my eyes and stubble on my chin did not disguise the smirk on Mouth. The phrase, "Fringe benefit," flashed across my mind. "Damn you, damn you to hell!" I hissed.

Mouth ceased to have a life of its own—no smirk, no more entangling agreements flowing forth. My face was now just the usual collection of ordinary but too often revealing features. For a few moments, I thought I should practice looking enigmatic, in view of the assignment Fate had presented me with. Yes, Fate was making me do it! Ah, yes, and Fate was sending me up some canyon to a brunch with a long-lost love. I shrugged as I picked up my electric razor and began to prepare Face for the day ahead. Another part of my anatomy seemed to be assuming a life of its own! I heard myself muttering, "Mouth, Face, Prick, don't get me into more trouble, please!" And then that corniest of corny phrases, "I'm too young to die!"

It's amazing how banalities can carry the ring of truth. That word 'die' suddenly struck real fear into my soul. It had not quite penetrated my befuddled brain during the past two days that I was really getting mixed up with a murderer. If I were to slip up in any way, so that Bob Wexler found out what I was really up to, I did not doubt that he would add me to his list of victims. He had ruthlessly killed at least twice in his pursuit of ends which had enabled him to achieve wealth and power. This second term in the Senate was presumably the opportunity to achieve further goals. "Build thee more stately mansions, O my soul, As the swift seasons roll! Leave thy low-vaulted past! Let each new temple, nobler than the last, Shut thee from heaven with a dome more vast,...." Why did lines from Oliver Wendell Holmes' "The Chambered Nautilus" come to mind in this situation, for heaven's sake? "Build me more stately mansions" was no doubt one of Bob Wexler's objectives, but his soul had gotten lost somewhere in the process. I'd probably see his latest earthly temple this afternoon, though I doubted that it would have a dome.

When I got down to the lobby, Marilou was waiting for me, resplendent in a bright-colored, low-cut blouse and tight skirt. There was no move for a kiss, either in friendly greeting or provocative invitation. I was glad. I didn't need to have that to cope with at the moment. We proceeded to the parking lot where Marilou found her car, a red, classy, late model sportscar. I was parked quite a distance from her, so she took me to my rented car. As I got out of her car, Marilou breezily said, "Just follow me. It'll take about three-quarters of an hour."

Any number of times during the next three-quarters of an hour I wished she had given me some specific directions so that I would not have had to keep her careening vehicle in sight. It had been years since I'd driven mountain roads, and the road up Marilou's canyon was no freeway! I'm basically your conservative driver at best and even more timid on mountain roads. But Marilou was hell on wheels, a real credit to women's lib, I suppose. Unfortunately, I had worn my suit coat and a necktie. By the time we turned off into a single-lane road that wound up to her place, beads of sweat were standing on my brow and my shirt was soaked.

It didn't take me very long to come to the conclusion that Marilou was a lot better off as a single professional woman than she would have been living with me as a faculty wife. The house was stunning. She had been engaged in a little temple building herself. Roofs came to dramatic points, glass walls gave magnificent views of the Front Range, terraces and decks wrapped around the place, soaring out in alarming fashion above the trees that grew on the steep slopes below. A spiral staircase wound from the two-story entrance foyer up to a balcony that looked down into the sunken living room below. Here a huge sandstone fireplace placed between two enormous picture windows that went floor to ceiling served as the focus of the several over-sized davenports and chairs, upholstered in earth-tones and accented with cushions the green color of the trees outside. Large, expensive Navajo rugs were scattered over the polished wood floors, and several tasteful *objets d'art* were placed in strategic niches or on small tables. The few wall spaces not used up by glass windows were used to display several excellent oils of western scenes, works which would have done credit to many a museum featuring Western art—The Denver Art Museum or the Indianapolis Eiteljorg Museum of Indian and Western Art, for instance. It was real class. "Great fringe benefit!" flashed into my mind, but I pushed the thought into the subconscious as best I could. Lucille and I have a few good pieces ourselves, back in Jeffreysville, chosen largely by Lucille, and quite contemporary, of course, considering her profession. But I was sure that any one of Marilou's paintings could bring more at auction than all the Moffett collection put together might.

There wasn't much time for contemplating the affluence of Marilou Baxter, however. She had ascended that spiral staircase with amazing alacrity, especially since she was carrying her suitcase. In a few moments she came cork screwing down again, now in very short shorts, and another low-cut blouse, blue and green and quite thin, to coordinate with the scenery, no doubt.

"Good God, you look hot, Don. Why'd you wear a coat and tie? Get into something comfortable. There are some shorts and sport shirts in the drawers in the chest in there. I'm pretty sure they'll fit. The owner isn't apt to be back for a while and will never know. Go make yourself presentable while I get going in the kitchen." She indicated a door off the foyer which led into a guest bedroom which seemed to be floating on air, judging from what I could see from the floor to ceiling window in the opposite wall. "There are towels in the bathroom, too, so take a shower if you want to cool off."

I docilely went into the bedroom and indeed found the clothing Marilou had indicated would be in the chest. There seemed to be a good supply of men's clothes, and I took a peek into the big walk-in closet and found several sports jackets and slacks there. I was rapidly coming to several conclusions about Marilou Baxter. It was apparent that not only was she well off financially, but she had not been living the sad and celibate life of a jilted woman carrying the memories of her youthful loves into dispirited old age. I found this surprisingly comforting. As I took a quick, cold shower, I realized that I somehow had been experiencing an uneasy feeling of guilt the last couple of days, possibly guilt for having sent Marilou off on that bus in New Haven twenty-four years ago, presumably never to be seen by me again. So the come-on she'd been giving me during the reunion was just for fun and games. Just possibly "fringe benefits," for Marilou as well as for me. Ah, that damn phrase again had flashed into my consciousness. I found myself muttering in my best Shakespearean voice, "Out, damn phrase! out, I say! One; two..." So now it was Shakespeare rather than Oliver Wendell Holmes! I'd had no idea my mind would turn even casually to literary lines, as commonplace as they were. Bemused by this bit of introspection, I dried myself, dressed in some unknown man's shorts and shirt, put on a pair of sandals that seemed more appropriate than my wing-tips, and returned to the main portion of the house.

The kitchen and dining area were on the opposite side of the foyer, and a railing separated the area from the sunken living room. Tantalizing smells were already emanating from the kitchen as I found my way into what had to be a decorator's *tour de force*. Gleaming pots of all sizes hung from a huge circular bracket suspended over a central, marble-topped work table. Baskets were lined up on top of the cabinets over the counters. A huge copper fridge dominated one wall, and somewhere in all this grandeur were stove, sinks, dishwasher, and compactor. In the midst of the splendor, Marilou was functioning with the elan of a professional chef.

"Take those things out to the table on the balcony, Don. I've already put a cloth on the table. I'll have the omelet and bacon ready in a few minutes, and the rolls will be done by then. Aren't frozen things wonderful? I could let you think I made the rolls from scratch, but I want to be honest with you. You'd probably figure out I didn't make them anyway."

I couldn't tell whether this was just a passing remark, or if it was perhaps a prelude to some revelations that would come with the second course. That there could be revelations was obvious. Whether I would be privy to them would remain to be seen. I gathered up a handful of blue-handled flat-ware and a couple of large blue and green napkins and took them out onto the dining balcony.

This afforded yet another spectacular view toward the rear of the house where a small but totally charming waterfall cascaded over great sandstone boulders. Four or five feet below this balcony was another larger one, opening off the living room, and to the right of that was a swimming pool, again precariously perched on the side of the steep slope. For a few moments I stood, transfixed by the loveliness of it all. The air was cool and crisp though the sun was shining brightly, and the smell of pines was heavy in the morning air. What a wonderful state, this mile-high Colorado! Well, this was a good bit higher than a mile high, judging from that climbing road we had just negotiated. The mile-high epithet referred to Denver. For one awful moment, I found myself thinking that I'd give anything, anything to live out here. And indeed Bob Wexler had offered me just that opportunity, and it might be an open-ended proposition if I chose to play my cards correctly. "Build thee more stately mansions, O my soul,...till thou at length art free, Leaving thine outgrown shell by life's unresting sea!" Ah, but I wouldn't be free. Far from it. Brown-nosing a murderer, prostituting my chosen profession, and abandoning my wife of more than twenty years. And abandon Lucille I would, I had no doubt. It would take a stronger character than I am to indefinitely resist the kind of temptation I was being offered on silver platters out here in the Silver State. A new literary allusion came to mind. Actually, the credit should be given to the composer Gounod, as I probably never would have known the Faust story were it not for his opera. At any rate, for the moment, I considered myself to be some noble Faustian character being sorely tempted by Mephistopheles—Bob Wexler?—to sell my soul for youth, epitomized by Colorado, cool, colorful, healthful Colorado. But this simile broke down, and I decided maybe I was Parsifal, the perfect fool, tempted by Kundry in the second act of that Wagnerian *tour de force*. Up to now, I had never considered myself to be a fool, perfect or otherwise. Being in an operatic mode, as it were, I decided perhaps Tannhaeuser might be a better choice, if I had to assume an operatic role, and this glorious mountain setting was my Venusberg.

At that moment, Venus arrived—Marilou, that is—pushing a tea cart laden with plates, cups and saucers, glasses of orange juice, a silver coffee pot emitting delicious, earthy smells, and a huge silver salver covered by a silver dome which presumably was protecting from the cool mountain air hot eggs, bacon, and rolls. In a few moments, I was succumbing to temptations much more immediate and mundane than those in my recent fantasies, namely the ingesting of Marilou's brunch. I realized that I was ravenous. The various meals served to us during the reunion festivities had been excellent, but each occasion had involved conversations and people that had made eating less than satisfactory. For the next half hour, I not once thought of my waist-line, of calories, or of cholesterol. In that respect, Mephistopheles had won the first round. Conversation was casual, Marilou doing most of the talking. She discussed the house, the people she had seen at the reunion, a book project she was working on, and a collection of rare books she was trying to persuade a wealthy collector to leave to the University. There was absolutely nothing of a personal nature, nor were there any revelations about her private life. When we were about half way through the brunch, she produced a wine bottle and glasses, remarking that Sunday brunch wasn't complete without champagne.

Then we had finished all the food, practically every morsel of it, and were sipping the last glass of champagne. As it had been at my first meeting with Amanda and Marilou, it appeared as though it was now up to me to introduce the next topic of conversation, and it seemed that it should be a topic of a personal, and possibly questionable, nature. I took the plunge.

"I'm glad not to be wearing my suit. I guess I'd put it on because it was Sunday morning or something. I could have gotten my own things out of my suitcase, of course, but it was handy having these things there in the guest room."

Marilou did not take the bait. She just looked at me with those astonishing blue eyes of hers, a sort of Mona Lisa smile on her lips. I had to carry on.

"I guess your last guest must have left in a hurry. I just hope he doesn't come roaring in and beat me up for having his clothes on and for having Sunday brunch with his..." I realized that I'd worked myself into an embarrassing corner. I was definitely at loss for a word, but I added lamely, "...his hostess."

At that, probably because of a look of embarrassment on my expressive face (damn Face!), Marilou broke into gales of laughter. It was a very pretty sound indeed, but my discomfort was in no way abated by that fact. Finally she got sufficient control of herself to talk.

"Oh, Don, you haven't changed a bit. You're the same sweet, naive guy I fell in love with twenty-seven years ago. I used to wonder if you ever would get more sophisticated. It worried me, especially after you were so, ah, reserved, about the physical side of the relationship. I told you yesterday that I even wondered if you were gay, you know. Only of course we didn't call it gay then. Queer was the word, I guess. But of course, I was naive too, or I'd have known why you acted the way you did. It would have saved me a lot of heart-break if I'd just understood. But as you can see, I've not spent my life pining away for you, or for Bob Wexler. I found that I could do many interesting things, meet many interesting people, and go many exciting places on my own. Oh, it is a bit awkward at times without a man in tow, but actually during the past several years even that little inconvenience has pretty much been dissipated by a more enlightened society. My love life has not been without its moments. I've always been careful, selective as it were, and discrete. And with this AIDS thing, it is even more important to be careful. You want to know whose clothes you are wearing, don't you? Your eyeballs look like big question marks! Well, they belong to my New York publisher who likes to come out for a bit of Colorado air and peace and quiet every so often...several times a year, as a matter of fact. There are absolutely no commitments. He is married to a woman who wouldn't be caught dead west of the Hudson River. She lives in a fifty-first floor penthouse but thinks that a mountain would be the most terrifying thing imaginable. Bert loves to hike in the summer and ski in the winter, and so do I. He helps me with my writing, I give him some periods of peace and quiet from the rat race of New York, and neither of us worry about what the other does in between times. If I decide to have a little fling with someone, say like a professor from the Midwest, no problem. I might tell him. I might not, if it didn't come up naturally. It isn't the perfect arrangement, I suppose, from the Victorian, conventional standpoint, but it works fine for a somewhat aggressive professional woman such as I. I simply couldn't handle a family, a perpetual man around the house wanting his sox washed, and at the same time be myself, the Marilou Baxter I've become.

If I'd started out my adult life in the conventional way, I'm sure that also would have been satisfactory, but Bob Wexler derailed me, and you didn't see fit to get me back on the track, so here I am—and isn't this simply grand?"

As she said that, Marilou made a sweeping gesture that encompassed her house and the entire Front Range. It all made sense—so very, very modern. But I thought of Lucille who had a husband, had raised a family, maintained a house and at the same time had pursued her career as a teacher of art history and sculpture and had created some very lovely things herself. So just a few minutes ago I'd been telling myself that I could abandon that for this? Now I told myself that I really would make an archetypical operatic tenor lead (except that I can't sing worth a damn). They are always straying from some faithful, deserving, innocent woman, tempted by some Carmen, or Kundry, or Venus or whomever, to be led to their doom and eternal damnation.

These observations seemed to get me back to reality, a state of mind that had been notably infrequent during the past three days. My musings were interrupted by Marilou, who had been looking at me with a quizzical expression.

"Well, thank heavens you don't look particularly shocked. I must say that you don't even look disappointed. You might at least have given me the satisfaction of being jealous. Hey, I take back what I said about your not having changed. You are more sophisticated than I'd given you credit for. That's good. I'll feel a lot more comfortable with you now, in bed or out of bed. And frankly, it's not that much of a deal. I just had thought it would be fun, and sort of wind things up, as it were. Finish off what didn't get finished twenty-five years ago."

After gaping at Marilou for a moment, I simply said "Amazing!" and then I leaned across the table and gave her a chaste kiss. "Now let's talk about my assignment to prove Bob Wexler was a murderer and see that he doesn't get elected to congress again. If you have any good ideas, I can use them. I feel pretty inadequate."

CHAPTER 9

The next two hours were pleasantly spent, just two old friends getting caught up on the news of twenty-five years past. There was none of the tension that had been so disturbing during the two days of the reunion. Having been frank about her lifestyle, Marilou now assumed a relaxed, laid-back attitude. I had the feeling that if I wanted to make a move, she'd be more than pleased to do her part. But if I didn't, that was O.K. also. I began to understand what Amanda had implied about Marilou's success in obtaining donors for the University's rare books collection. She was smooth, charming, intelligent, and imaginative. She had developed a fine sense of humor, a sort of detached observation of humanity in general, of people in particular, and of herself. I found this most engaging. I could imagine that she would be able to talk almost anyone into or out of anything she chose. During one very brief lull in the conversation, as we both contemplated the remaining patches of gleaming snow on the highest peaks of the Front Range, I decided that if she had a mind to, she could indeed talk me into her bed. However, I've since been eternally grateful that she did not choose to do so. I was spared the need to carry a baggage of guilt for the rest of my life with Lucille, back on the campus of DeMott University. As it is, if I don't think too hard about it, I can take complete credit for my faithfulness to my wife and can be smugly censorious of my friends and colleagues who have not been so honorable in adhering to their marriage vows. Not that at that moment I was thinking that far ahead. I guess Fate had decided to take my side, for a change.

Then it was time to leave for Denver. Marilou told me to leave the clothes on the bed in the guest room. She said she'd have them laundered before Bert came again. She said something about his coming before the end of the month for a stay of several weeks. I changed back into my own clothes, skipping the necktie and jacket. At the door, Marilou gave me a good bye kiss, not a passionate kiss but not a cold one either.

"Take care of yourself, Don. Please be careful. Bob Wexler is a bad one. I'd hate to have anything happen to you. I still love you, you know, in my own way."

After getting into the car, I sat a few moments, contemplating this last remark. Then I looked at my maps, figured out what the best route down to Denver would be, and swung out of the driveway as Marilou stood at the door waving.

The drive down the canyon was considerably more leisurely than the trip up to Marilou's house had been. I was still feeling the effects of the champagne a bit, and I didn't want to foul things up now with a DUI ticket. Then I was through the foothills, and after a little while, I picked up Interstate 25 which runs along the base of the Rockies. When I got near the outskirts of Denver, I turned off and stopped at a gas station. I again consulted my map and the card with the Wexler address on it that Jessamin had given me. I finally figured out where I was going and how I'd get there, and I decided it would be smart to have my accommodations for Sunday night taken care of before meeting the Wexlers. Going over to a phone booth (where wonder of wonders there was a phone directory), I looked up the address of an Embassy Suite Hotel out on East Hampden and gave the hotel a call to be sure they would have accommodations for me. Though not exactly near the Wexler's, it was at least on the right side of the city. I had not known Denver all that well when I was in college, but I was pretty sure this area had been way out in the country in those days.

Interstate 25 goes right through the heart of the city, and I was continually amazed at how the city had changed since I had last seen it. Skyscrapers of the down-town business section soared into the smoggy sky, and the infrequent building I might recognize as I sped past on the freeway had seemingly shrunk with the passing years, not that I remembered those many landmarks.

I'd never stayed at an Embassy Suites before, though of course I'd read their ads. When I had checked in and had gone to my suite, I found that the accomodations were nice, but I had a hunch that I was going to feel pretty lonesome rattling around in the two big rooms.

Having freshened up a bit and put on a clean shirt, I took off to find my way to the Wexler's. They were in a posh development in an area that I knew had been nothing but sagebrush and prairie grass twenty-five years before. I had expected a house something on the order of Marilou's, but this was not the case. The place was big and expensive, but imaginative it was not. It has been my observation that when houses get beyond a certain size, it becomes very difficult to make them both architecturally valid and also attractive. The builders of the stately homes in England and the chateaus in France as a rule managed to do it with a flair, but in the case of the Wexler pad, the architect had missed the boat. It was brick, with some Georgian pillars across the front. The shutters on each side of all the windows merely emphasized the fact that there were too many windows in the flat facade to be attractive. There was a big lawn of course, but the landscaping had not that first personal touch about it. Bob and Jessamin obviously had things to think about other than making an attractive home for themselves. Or perhaps they just had indifferent tastes.

A white-coated young oriental man answered the door chime and ushered me into a wide central hall and through double doors at the far end. A flight of steps led down to a large swimming pool, on the opposite side of which was a cabana. Well, not exactly a cabana; maybe it was more like a Greek temple—a Georgian Greek temple. Oh, give it up! It was a nondescript architectural conceit, but it did provide shelter from the hot afternoon sun. That much I can say for it. In the center of the monstrosity was a *chaise longue*, and draped on that was Jessamin. She motioned to me to come around the pool, and the white-coated house man silently disappeared. As I made my way around the pool and up the three steps into the temple, I was

Oswald G. Ragatz

painfully aware of the careful scrutiny of Jessamin's almond-shaped green eyes. I suddenly felt as though my clothes had been purchased at a Goodwill store, and for the first time in my life, I wondered how I looked when I walked. Why I should have worried about MY clothes remains a mystery, since Jessamin at first gave the impression of having absolutely nothing on. As I got nearer, however, it became apparent that she was wearing the briefest of bikinis and a bra that neither disguised or supported anything. Actually, nature had taken care of the matter of support most admirably, or was it the result of cosmetic surgery?.

Jessamin extended her hand to me.

"So good to see you again, Don. Sit down and have a drink. I'm having gin and tonic. Is that O.K.?"

As I settled myself in a lounge chair, I indicated that the gin and tonic would be fine. Jessamin picked up a portable phone and in a moment was ordering two drinks.

"The rest of them aren't here yet. You'll have to get used to their being late. It's a point of honor with my dad and my uncle to always keep people waiting. My brother Larry is usually late because he's lazy and disorganized, and of course Bob wouldn't break with family tradition. Bob is bringing Ron Dawson, his campaign manager. They had another meeting earlier this afternoon down at the Brown Palace Hotel. So that leaves just the two of us, and isn't this nice?"

I wasn't sure whether that was a question to be answered or not, but fortunately I didn't have to decide since at that moment the white-coated one materialized from somewhere with two tall, frosted glasses of gin and tonic. I decided that some conventional civilities were in order.

"You have a lovely place here," I lied bravely.

Jessamin's eyebrows arched, and those penetrating eyes sent the message, "You jest!" But her voice was silky smooth.

"Yes, well, Bob likes it. I'd prefer something more, more personal. But Bob says he had all the artsy fartsy decor he could tolerate in one lifetime during his last marriage. His last wife

Tillie was a sometime artist, as you may know, and I gather was quite a collector of what Bob calls Objets d'Fart. He can be quite cruel some times, if you let it get to you. I don't. You'll not find me committing suicide because of Bob Wexler! Not that I would have any reason to do so, you understand. Quite to the contrary. He's handsome, socially acceptable, a good lover when he gets around to it, and is very, very useful to the VonBronigans. And I don't have a jealous bone in my body—I couldn't afford to." Did I detect a slight leer at this last comment?

This matter-of-fact candor, with just an undercurrent of acidity, threw me off balance. This wasn't quite the adoring-wife image Jessamin had projected at the banquet the night before. I could think of no rejoinder, nor was it necessary, as Jessamin was continuing.

"And speaking of the VonBronigans, let me clue you in to each and every one of them. By the way, I find that their lack of punctuality is very useful at times. It gives me an opportunity to get the real business out of the way. Now there is my dad, ex criminal lawyer *par excellence* and one of the sharpest entrepreneurs of the century. Uncle Karl is three years older than Dad, not quite as smart, but twice as crooked, if that's possible. The two of them hate each other, I do believe, but they work together hand in glove. It's a formidable combination. Then there's my brother Larry, lazy, a drunk, gay, and maybe just plain dumb. I've never figured out whether he has a brain or not. But oh, so charming! Much of the time we get on quite well. We have certain interests in common—financial interests, that is. When Dad and Uncle Karl are gone, it will be up to Larry and me to hold the empire together. And that means it will be up to me. Larry has no sense, business or otherwise. The old men know this, of course, and that's why Dad was so interested in having Bob come into the family. Bob had done legal work for the VonBronigans when he was with the Bauer firm. His association with Bauer and Company is on hold now that he's in the Senate, and that's where the VonBronigans come in. Bob has been very useful in a number of ventures we have been involved in. We had acquired a lot of land out toward Aurora, some time before it became public knowledge that a new international airport would possibly be built out there. It took a lot of pushing and propaganda to get that through, and Bob's contacts in Washington were invaluable, with the C.A.A. and for government financing. We've made a bundle on the project. It has taken Bob a while to make the necessary connections in Washington, but he now is on the Inside, and it is absolutely necessary that he get reelected. The big water project, the Two Forks Dam which would impound water of the South Platte river for use in the metropolitan area, is meeting with a lot of problems. The environmentalists along with sportsmen—hunters and fishermen—are raising hell about the project. In the meantime, we have a lot of money tied up in land which will become very valuable once the dam is built, and we own several companies that will no doubt be involved in the construction itself. And by the way, these same companies were also involved in building the airport. Bob can probably get the E.P.A. to see things our way if he gets back to Washington. Then there's another project that will make the environmentalists yell when they find out about it, a combination ski resort and condo development, a sort of little Aspen on the Eastern Slope. That one is really tricky because we've gone ahead with a lot of the building without the proper permits. It's on land that was originally a mining company claim. We got control of the company, so we have title to the land. But there are problems involving water and land usage. I think it was dumb to start building before everything was in order, but Uncle Karl was for it and couldn't wait to get started. He is so sure Bob will get reelected and will work everything out. Actually, it was Bob's idea in the first place. I've not seen the site, but it's a place Bob knew because there's skiing late in the season and early in the fall, as well as in the winter—a sort of small glacier, I believe. He said he used to go skiing up there."

Reunion With Murder

I felt antennas sprouting from my head at the mention of skiing and a small glacier. I hoped that Jessamin didn't notice my excitement.

Again I was spared having to comment by the arrival of someone. This time it was Jessamin's father and uncle. It seemed to be a foregone conclusion that the meeting would be in the structure at the far end of the pool. The two men carefully lumbered their way past the deck chairs. By the time introductions were made and they had found places to sit, the oriental man had arrived with drinks—double Scotch and sodas for both the old men.

A moment later the brother arrived. He rather floated around the pool. I almost expected him to take a short cut across the water, toes barely touching the surface. He was tall, had the same golden hair and green eyes as Jessamin, but the effect was not nearly as satisfactory as it was with her. He was just too pretty. His hair was cut almost as long as his sister's, and his fingers were as long and as white as were hers. He was indeed charming in an effeminate way, but I found myself being quite uncomfortable as he held my hand much too long during the introductory handshake.

Another drink was brought, this time something tall, pink, and with green sticking out of the top, for Larry, of course. The white-coated young oriental servant surely knew the taste of his regulars.

Larry had hardly commented on "this Gawd-awful summer heat" when Bob Wexler and his manager arrived. Bob, handsome as ever, was decked out in a white embroidered Philippine Guayabera shirt, white slacks and white loafers. His manager, Ronald Dawson, was looking very uncomfortable in a light colored suit and tie. He was a rather dumpy man, nearly a foot shorter than Bob Wexler. Watery blue eyes and thinning hair (thinner than mine, I was glad to see) gave him a somewhat ineffectual appearance.

When all introductions had been made and the newcomers were seated and drinks served (Bob and Dawson had Coors beer), conversation should have gotten underway. It was Larry who broke the momentary silence, and not very tactfully.

"Jess, darling, don't you think you should put some clothes on? Ron and Mr. Moffett are going to split their jock straps if you don't stop advertising."

The two older men looked bored, Ron Dawson blushed, and Jessamin looked daggers at her brother. Her retort dripped pure vitriol.

"I didn't know you disapproved of advertising, Larry dear. But I suppose when business is so good, you don't have to advertise."

Larry's green eyes opened very wide and his lips pouted.

"OOOh, did I say somesing awful? Do forgive Li'l Larry. I'm not very smart at times." He lit an extra long cigarette.

A loud grunt from Uncle Karl and an, "Oh, shut up Larry," from his dad did not creat a pleasant atmosphere. But Jessamin did get up from the lounge and go over to a sort of clothes rack in the corner where she retrieved a flimsy hostess coat of sorts. It didn't really hide much, but it was a gesture in the direction of modesty.

I looked at Bob to see how he was reacting to all of this, but he was sort of beaming at Larry with a benevolent smile on his face, no displeasure or disgust showing at all. What a dissembler the Senator was! Or was he really fond—maybe too fond—of his brother-in-law? I began to wonder.

When Jessamin had settled herself on her lounge again, Bob turned to her and said, "My dear, I assume you've had a chance to fill Don in on our family before we all got here?"

Jessamin had recovered her aplomb, and smiling adoringly at her husband, she answered, "Well, I tried. We'd not want him to be scared off, now would we? We need him too much."

This seemed to be the cue to get the conversation on track, and for the next two hours politics and strategies were discussed. Larry took very little part in the conversation. He would periodically get up and wander around the pool, and finally he actually took off all his clothes and dived in, swimming expertly for several laps, and then sunning himself dry on the deck nearest the house. That was the only time the conversation didn't deal with the business at hand. Jessamin snarled bitterly, "And he had the nerve to tell me to put on some clothes! Talk about advertising!" Then we were back to devising approaches to the Hispanic population of the metropolitan area. For the first hour or so I mostly listened, getting the lay of the land, as it were. Initially, I felt very insecure, but little by little I saw where some intelligent guidance would not be amiss, and I felt that I could make some contributions.

The VonBronigan solution to every problem could be called the bulldozer approach. "If they don't like what we are doing or what we want, we plow 'em under!" Bob and Dawson were considerably more realistic, but neither of them really had any true grasp of how to go about getting votes from the laboring classes, and especially the Hispanics. I began to suggest, and then to insist, that the Wexler campaign had to promise these people something tangible, something for their own pockets or bellies, or for their families. I began to ask about the educational system in the city, and I was dismayed to find that Bob was singularly unaware of any details of what actually existed. He looked bored when I mentioned minimum wage scales. He had some figures on unemployment for certain segments of the state's population, figures which were rather shocking, but he had no specific promises to make to alleviate the situation other than the Two Forks Dam project. Granted that that would employ a good many people, were it to come about, but there was a large segment of voters who were farmers whose water would be preempted by the city usage of the impounded water. A lot of these people were Hispanics—lumped in the jargon of those present as "Those Mexicans," which, of course, many of them are—and orientals who came to Colorado during the evacuation of the oriental population of the West Coast during World War II.

I kept wondering how Bob had gotten elected to his first term in the Senate, with no more definite program to offer than

Oswald G. Ragatz

was now evident. However, this question was answered in part by some remarks made by his dad. "Too bad your opponent is so squeaky-clean this time."

Uncle Karl added, "I doubt if we can pin anything on him the way we took care of that bastard running against you last time. It would be pretty hard to hang a drug rap on The Reverend." After a bit, I deduced that the opponent was not actually a minister, but that he was a churchman with a high moral reputation. The term Reverend was their way of showing their scorn for the man.

I actually became immersed in the discussion so thoroughly that I forgot my real goal—setting up Bob Wexler so that he would face two murder raps. The realities of this sort of political activity were a far cry from the text-book, class-room consideration of political theories. I found it intriguing, enlightening, disillusioning, and thoroughly stimulating. I knew I'd return to DeMott University a better teacher—if I ever returned to teaching!

The afternoon was cooling off rapidly. Larry had dressed himself, and periodically would float into our group, listen a few moments, and likely as not would make some inane, rather snide remark before wandering off again. The most constructive suggestions by far were made by Jessamin, usually then seconded by Bob and his manager. The older generation often seemed more interested in the refills of their drinks and their cigars. But when they did make remarks, they were aggressive, focused on money, and quite insensitive to the needs and situations of the "little people" who would cast the votes. I could certainly see why Bob Wexler had latched on to me. Ron Dawson had some good ideas now and then, but his personality was such that it always seemed doubtful that the ideas could be implemented. After two hours, I laid out an agenda for myself which would start with some digging in the library on Monday. I had to inform myself about a number of issues, from the airport to the Two Forks Dam, to say nothing of the general political and economic situation the state.

Bob seemed pleased that I was taking a hold of things, and he slapped me on the back with a "I knew you'd be able to do it, Old Buddy!" I did not think Jessamin looked as certain, but she gave me one of those dazzling smiles and murmured, "We'll try, won't we, Don?"

The white-coated oriental man, who had been keeping the drinks fresh, now announced that supper would be served in ten minutes. The VonBronigan brothers hoisted themselves out of their chairs and trudged off toward the house. As the group broke up, Bob put his hand on Larry's shoulder and they moved off toward the house, talking in low voices to one another. I offered my hand to Jessamin to help her get up off the lounge, since no one else had extended her that courtesy. She did not release my hand after she was standing, however, so we went toward the house hand in hand, like old friends. Poor Ron Dawson tagged along behind. I would have given anything to have seen the look on his face, but, of course, I couldn't very well turn around. As for my Face? I didn't dare think of what it might be revealing.

CHAPTER 10

Jessamin showed me to a lavatory off the entrance hall so that I could "freshen up," while the others went on up the stairs. I emerged from the gold and green confines of the powder room to find the house seemingly deserted. I wandered into the cavernous living room with its department-store display-room ambience. Expensive and sterile would best describe the decor—certainly not my taste. After a bit, the two senior VonBronigans came in, polluting the air with fresh cigars. Then Ron Dawson apologetically appeared, followed by Jessamin in a low-cut dinner gown of apricot-colored crepe. It was some time before Bob and Larry came in, Bob looking pleased with life, or at least with himself, Larry drifting about in an even more languid manner than usual. Jessamin moved to my side and steered me toward the dining room on the opposite side of the hall. Ron said something to Bob in reference to some topic of earlier conversation. The VonBronigan seniors put out their cigars and followed Jessamin and me across the hall. Larry went over to a sideboard where several liquor bottles stood and poured himself a large drink which he had downed by the time he wafted into the dining-room.

Jessamin seated me to her right, with Uncle Karl on my right. Bob sat at the far end of the long, Queen Anne table, with Larry on his right, Ron Dawson on his left. A uniformed Chicano woman and the oriental man served the meal—excellent chicken salad, hot rolls, some sort of tomato aspic salad, all accompanied by superb wine. Conversation was desultory at first, but then Karl began to tell me about the development of the ski resort. It was the first time he had shown much enthusiasm about anything. However, he clearly was completely wrapped up in this project. The more I heard about it the more I realized what an enormous risk they were taking. It was obvious that much of the work was far along, even though some of the crucial permits had not been obtained. The ski lift itself was in place, forty condominium units were already under roof, and sixty more were begun. A large recreation center was well under way. The excavation and grading for an Olympic-sized swimming pool had been completed, and a number of service buildings were finished, now already in use by construction crews. Land was being cleared for the first nine-holes of the golf course. It was obvious that timber had been clear-cut for the ski slopes and the golf course, as well as for the building sites and roads. Mention was made of the plan to utilize the small natural glacier as the basis of a spectacular ski-jump. If this were being done where I thought it probably was, I assumed that something was being done about the jagged rocks at the end of the glacier!

During her uncle's monologue, Jessamin looked worried and disapproving. She occasionally glanced at Bob and Larry, who were engaged in animated conversation, and at such moments her face displayed considerable distaste and boredom. It was becoming obvious that the clubby rapport between her husband and her brother did not please her. Ron Dawson and Jessamin's father had little or nothing to say throughout the meal.

When the desert was being served—some sort of exotic Italian ice cream—Bob's attention became focused on his uncle's description of his vision of his Little Aspen on the Eastern Slope. I happened to glance at Bob, probably because the murmur of his conversation with Larry had stopped, and I found him looking at me with a questioning look just as Uncle Karl was talking about the ski jump and the glacier. I got the distinct impression that some new idea had just occurred to Bob. I decided that it may well have been the first time he had associated me with Jones Peak and the glacier. The episode which remained so clearly in my mind no doubt had been largely forgotten by him. And well it might, in view of the more momentous event that had transpired at that spot a year or so later. After all, I had survived, but Jake had not.

This was actually the first time during the afternoon that I had thought about my reason for being there. I can not describe the feeling of foreboding that swept over me at that moment. This crazy thing with which I had become involved could not possibly work. I would surely be the looser, a big looser, like being shipped back to Lucille in a box. I found myself morbidly wondering just what sort of "box" was used to ship bodies home. How was it done? U.P.S., freight, cross-country truck, C.O.D.?

My dismay must have been obvious but seemingly was misinterpreted by Bob. Or was it?

"Don't worry, Don, we'll be able to get those loose ends taken care of, especially when you help get us back to Washington. Those Sunday hikers and the stupid fishermen won't have a chance once I get to my pals at the E.P.A. So which is more important, happy skiers or happy fishermen? Skiers will bring us a lot more money than a catch of trout, and more votes too." And he burst into hearty laughter.

After we finished the meal, Jessamin, Bob, Ron, and I went into the library. I wondered how many of the books Bob had read. We discussed what I might be expected to do during the next week while Bob was in Washington. We decided that I would be involved with studying the background of Colorado politics. Especially would I inform myself with all the crucial issues of the moment. These centered mostly around water, land use, conservation of other natural resources, plus unemployment and low income levels for sizeable segments of the working population of the state. It was assumed by the others that I would come up with ideas as to how we could defuse the opposition and win votes. I said something about going through back issues of the local newspapers, the Rocky Mountain News and the Denver Post. At the mention of the Post, Bob emitted a snort of derision, and indicated that I'd better not count on what that "pink rag," as he called it, had to say about anything.

I was becoming very tired, and the other three seemed increasingly to have other matters on their minds. It was obviously time for me to depart. I shook hands with Bob and Ron Dawson, and Jessamin led me from the library to a small room at the back of the house where her father and uncle were watching television. The two men were engrossed in their show, so civilities of my departure were brief. Larry was nowhere to be seen as Jessamin took me to the door.

"Well, now you have seen us at our best." Jessamin sounded cynical. "You will no doubt see some of us at our worst before this is over. I may be unduly pessimistic, but I am not sure that you or anyone else is going to get this reelection to work. I have my fingers crossed that some of the VonBronigan machinations won't come to light and implicate Bob. And his own past hasn't been all that squeaky clean, you know. I like you, Don, but you may be too honest to do us much good. It's really quite refreshing to talk to someone like you, but in business and in politics, survival usually goes to the meanest, not necessarily to the fittest. Well, we'll see."

She turned up her face to me for a kiss, which I thought was a bit too enthusiastic considering our relationship.

I took my time getting back to the Embassy Suites, and as a matter of fact, I got lost twice before getting onto a major thoroughfare which I recognized. Bob had given me the address of the building where my duplex was, in anticipation of my taking possession on Monday. I had originally looked forward to that experience, but now I found myself dreading the move into a VonBronigan building. The impersonal Embassy Suites was, at the moment, very attractive. I was finding that anything connected with Bob Wexler or the VonBronigans was taking on a sinister aspect. The VonBronigan wheelings and dealings and total disregard for the human consequences, to say nothing of Bob's presumed perpetration of two murders, made me most uncomfortable—an understatement indeed!

Back in my hotel suite, I was about to hit the hay when I remembered that I should get in contact with Hank Davis. Amanda answered after the second ring.

"Don, where are you? We've been wondering if you had escaped the clutches of Marilou and Jessamin." Her lilting voice was infused with humor. But I detected an undercurrent of seriousness too. I tried to answer in the same vein.

"Not to worry, except following Marilou up that canyon road about did me in. Her place is certainly beautiful, and we settled into a comfortable, no-stress three hours of catching up on our lives."

Amanda's reply sounded relieved. "There certainly has been some electricity flashing between you two the past two days. I can't say whether I approved or disapproved. It just would complicate things immensely if you were to get sidetracked by some romantic entanglement. Now, how about Jessamin, the green-eyed *femme fatale?*"

I could answer that one very frankly.

"For me she poses no temptation of a carnal nature. She is one calculating, formidable iron woman. Frightening, really, and about as amoral as they come, I'd say. I was with all the VonBronigans for about five hours. Bob was his usual self-assured, shallow self. His campaign manager is intelligent but ineffectual. He doesn't have a chance against all those other strong personalities. Jessamin's father and uncle are ruthless, and I think not always very smart. And then there is limp-wristed Larry. Now what is the story on him? He sure seems to be a, a... ."

Amanda's laugh interrupted me. "A flaming gay? That he is, and notorious about town. But there are those who think he is the smartest of them all, if his hormones wouldn't keep getting him in trouble. I personally rather question this evaluation, though he could just be putting on a big act, waiting for an opportunity to implement some plan giving him control of the family fortune."

I found myself verbalizing an idea that had been lurking in the back of my mind since I had watched Bob and Larry go into the house before supper, Bob's hand on Larry's shoulder.

"Has there ever been any talk about Bob's being bisexual, or having a thing for his wife's brother?"

Amanda didn't answer immediately. In fact, I wondered if the connection had been broken. When she finally spoke, there was considerable acrimony in her voice.

Reunion With Murder

"You forget that I was married to the louse for five years. No, I've never heard anything about Larry and Bob, nor would I, since we don't exactly move in the same circles, you know. But, yes, I had my suspicions about my dear ex-husband on the subject of his fondness for those of his own sex on a number of occasions. Nothing I could prove—just a gut reaction."

My reply was matter of fact.

"Well, that's something that will be interesting to watch. Now I had better talk to Hank, if he's there. It's good to talk to you, Amanda. You're so, so down to earth."

"I try to be, Don. Hold on, here's Hank," was her reply.

For the moment, Hank's confident, cheery voice pushed my recent doubts to the back of my mind.

"So you had quite a day, Don. I listened in on the extension to your conversation with Amanda. I hope you don't mind."

"Of course not. It saves saying things over," I answered. But I reminded myself never to say anything to Amanda on the phone that I wouldn't want Hank to hear. Characteristically, Hank was taking complete charge of the conversation.

"What are your plans for tomorrow, or for the rest of the week, for that matter?"

I explained briefly my need to do considerable research so I would know, as they say, where I was coming from. I explained that Wexler would be back in Washington until the next weekend, and that I'd be working with Ron Dawson and probably Jessamin, though the latter hadn't been explicitly stated at any time. Wexler had some speaking engagement in Denver the following Saturday, and Dawson and I would have to have a good speech put together by then. Hank was all business.

"That's fine. Let them think you are doing their job for them. And I know you will do it well. We'll just assume that sooner or later something will come up that will enable us to derail the campaign, if indeed not to convict our friend Bob as a murderer. Now in the meantime, I'd like to see that Jones Peak and glacier, and I'd like to have you go with me. I called a friend of mine who is in the Rocky Mountain Hiking Club, and I have instructions on how to get to the place. It is really off the beaten path, as you said. He said there's a rumor that there is some sort of development going on up there, but no one seems to know much about it. Why don't you meet me for lunch tomorrow? We'll just casually encounter one another at the Tandoor Restaurant, on Blake Street, a couple of blocks down from Larimer Square. Then we can drive up to the mountains and get an idea of the lay of the land. Of course, it may be different from what it was twenty-six years ago. You can get away for an afternoon, can't you?"

I indicated that indeed there was something going on up there! And I told him a bit of what Uncle Karl had said about his project. Then I explained about moving into the new digs—duplex—pent house? But the suggestion of a trip to Jones Peak the next day seemed to be feasible. Hank ended the conversation.

"Maybe by then I will have more information from my friend in Washington. We're going to track down Wexler's charges for flights and car rentals on his American Express card, but as I said before, that probably will necessitate some legal procedures. But Joe will know. I'll see you tomorrow at lunch at twelve then?"

I assured Hank that I would indeed see him tomorrow, and we hung up.

I considered trying to call Lucille, but it was too late, even Denver time, so I had a good excuse to just take a short shower and fall into bed. I wondered if I'd have trouble sleeping, but I needn't have worried. I was exhausted from the marathon communication with high-powered and abrasive human beings throughout the long day, to say nothing of the several hours with Marilou and the mountain driving. In minutes I was sound asleep.

It was well after eight o'clock when I awoke the next morning. I barely made the breakfast smorgasboard at the hotel. Revived by rest and food, I was ready to face the world without too many misgivings.

Reunion With Murder

It was nearly eleven when I presented myself to the manager at the downtown high-rise where I would be living for the next several weeks or months. He called an assistant, who had me park in the building's underground garage. Then he ushered me up to my quarters on the top floor. It was a two-level affair. A large living room with a picture window toward the mountains, dinette, kitchen and small guest room were on the first level. A winding staircase led to the sumptuous master bedroom and bath on the upper level. Both these rooms opened out onto terraces which gave spectacular views of the city. The Larimer Square area was partly visible, and a little farther west, over on Sixteenth Street, one could see the remaining tower of the old Daniels and Fishers Department Store.

I hardly had time to get unpacked before it was time to leave for my luncheon date with Hank. It was several blocks to Blake street, but the morning was still cool, and the air remarkably clear, so I decided to walk to our meeting place. Parking no doubt would have been impossible. It was a bit past twelve when I finally arrived at the Tandoor Restaurant. At first I didn't see Hank, but then I heard someone call out, "Don, Don Moffett isn't it?"

There was Hank, coming from a table somewhat apart from others, looking surprised and hearty. He shook my hand and asked me how I'd been, as though he hadn't seen me for ages.

"Come on over and join me. I'm alone and would enjoy having a chance to talk to you."

Bemused by this subterfuge, and wondering if there could be anyone that mattered watching, I played along with Hank. He ordered martinis for us and suggested I should try the luncheon buffet. I wasn't hungry after my big breakfast, so I ordered a salad and a cup of soup.

Conversation was definitely general. Hank was obviously carrying the casual-meeting charade to the bitter end. We were nearly finished with our food when two men at a nearby table stood up, nodded to Hank, and went on out of the restaurant.

"I guess I could have chosen a better place to meet. Those two guys are staunch political supporters of our incumbent Senator, and they know me slightly. They know where I stand, so I didn't want to arouse any curiosity as to my association with you, in case they encounter you sometime in the future and remember seeing you here. Next time I'll think of a better place to meet."

I was skeptical. "I doubt if they would remember me. And anyway, what if they did?"

"That's just the point. We just happen to meet. I know lots of people, so they'd think nothing about it. I made a point of keeping the conversation general, just in case anything were overheard."

Hank picked up the tab for my lunch, and we were out on the sidewalk before anything more was said. Hank shook my hand as though we were taking leave of one another. But at the same time he said, "I'll meet you on the corner of Larimer and Eighteenth Street in twenty minutes. There's a loading zone where I can swing in just before the corner. We'll head for the mountains then. You can kill a little time wandering around Larimer Square till then. What they've done to the old buildings is quite interesting."

With that, Hank took off at a trot, presumably to retrieve his car from some parking place. I took his advice and wandered in an uptown direction to Larimer Street, where indeed there was enough to keep me occupied for fifteen minutes, and then some! I found that I was actually enjoying this mild cloak and dagger game. Then I reminded myself that it was no game, and I had better not enjoy it too much!

CHAPTER 11

We crept our way through traffic over to Twentieth Street and west across the viaduct and shortly picked up Interstate 25 going south. It was only four or five exits before we switched to Interstate 70 and headed toward the mountains. There was very little that looked familiar to me, though of course I hadn't known Denver all that well even when I was in school. We didn't get to the city very often, and when we did it was just to some specific place, like to a game or a concert or a show.

As soon as we got out of the city, Hank began to talk, and my attention to the route we were taking was sporadic. I knew that sometime after we had gotten through the foot-hills and into the mountains proper, we swung off the Interstate. After two or three more turns, we were on a little-traveled road, and we were doing considerable climbing that required second, and even at times, low gear. Hank had studied his map carefully and obviously knew exactly where he was going.

During this time, Hank's running commentary was most enlightening. Of course, it dealt chiefly with the need to defeat Bob Wexler in the senatorial campaign. This necessitated consideration of those problems faced by the state, and especially those problems which Hank felt would not be of sufficient concern for Bob were he to be reelected. For the most part, Hank's reasoning seemed sound. I found myself agreeing with him on almost every point. But I had to admit that during the previous afternoon there had been times when Bob's comments about what his campaign should or should not convey to the voters also had seemed sound. Now I found that I was having to face up to the fact that there often were two seemingly valid sides to some of the crucial issues. My academician's analytical approach to such problems was coming into play. I had to admit to myself that some of the precepts I had espoused in my class lectures had not practically addressed issues as I was finding them here in the real world. The problems involved in the proposed Two Forks Dam project was the best example of the sort of dichotomy which I was facing. If water were to be supplied for the burgeoning population of Denver, Aurora, Arvada and the other satellite cities, then that water would not be available to fill the reservoirs of the South Platte Valley later to be available for the farms during the summer growing season. Both needed the water. During those years when there was less than normal snowfall on the Eastern Slope, who should have priority? This involved legal and moral precepts which would require a Solomon to sort out. Of course, Bob was on the side of the VonBronigans, who favored the dam because of its impact on their industrial interests. Also, their land-holdings seemed to be concentrated chiefly in the metropolitan area. Hank, on the other hand, was taking the part of those who felt that the farmers in the rich, agricultural region of the Northeastern part of the state had first priority on the water. Other issues were equally perplexing when one looked at both sides. I was even reminded of Bob's glib remark about fisherman vs. skiers.

On the matter of Uncle Karl's Little Aspen project, I could feel much more comfortable. I am definitely a conservationist, and if the project was despoiling as much natural habitat as I had a hunch it was, then I was against it, to say nothing of their beginning the project without legal sanctions. This was just a good example of the VonBronigan's arrogant disregard for law and order and the commonweal. But this was not one of the major issues with which Hank was dealing, not yet, anyway.

What did become clear to me during the hour and half before we reached our destination was that true objectivity is a rare human trait. Hank was totally convinced that his stand on all matters was the only right one, and often it probably was just that. But there seemed to be no room for weighing the arguments of the other side. I began to understand my own dilemma for what it really was. Bob expected me to devise methods to sell him to the electorate, which meant sell his (or the VonBronigan) stand on the issues. Hank, on the other hand, was assuming that I was committed to scuttling the campaign by some magical discovery of an Achilles heel in our adversary.

It was at this point that I finally saw something out of the window that I recognized. For the most part (and I would never admit this to a true Coloradoan) except for the really notable peaks, like Pike's Peak or Long's Peak or Mount Evans, mountains all looked about the same to me. But suddenly through a break in the trees, I saw the outlines of Jones Peak up ahead, and there was a definite feeling of recognition that I had seen it before. I was back twenty-six years on a fall afternoon, riding with Bob Wexler as we drove up for our camp-out. And now I knew that it didn't matter whether or not I agreed with Hank or with the VonBronigans; my real job was to see that justice was done for murder. Understand, I had periodically come back to this point during the past three days, of course, but then I'd lose track of this all-important goal in the confusion and excitement of the new life into which I'd plunged. This time, though, I felt that the message was loud and clear in my mind. I promised myself that henceforth I would not loose sight of the real goal.

It was not long after this that Hank turned into a narrow, winding road, obviously more heavily traveled than it had ever been intended to be. A cloud of dust up ahead indicated that some major assault on the terrain was in progress, and we began to hear the rumble of heavy, earth-moving machines. Then suddenly we turned a bend in the lane, and we were stopped by a formidable gate set in a high chain-link fence. A glowering giant of a man in boots and plaid shirt emerged from a little booth and approached the car. There was no attempt to disguise the revolver in the holster at his side.

"This is strictly private property. No one's admitted. See that sign up there?" There was no attempt at civility in his voice, only threat. Indeed there was a large posted sign indicating that this was Private Property. As the man scrutinized both of us, Hank turned on his considerable charm.

"We just wanted to see how things were coming along. What we have heard about it indicates that it's a very interesting project. We just thought we'd like to see it first hand."

The guard looked at us coldly for a moment and then replied in the same gruff tone of voice he had used at first.

"It's interesting, alright. And you'll just have to continue hearing about it. There's no admittance unless you have a written statement from the proper people. And I assume you don't have such, or you'd have showed it to me right off. Now bug off. We ain't lettin' nobody nose around up here, understan'?"

His hand had rested menacingly on the holster at his side. Obviously this was one no-nonsense bully, just the sort of man people like the VonBronigans might hire to do their leg work.

Hank's smile showed all of his teeth but absolutely no humor as he said a thank you. He threw the car into gear and swung around, purposely throwing up a cloud of dust which enveloped the guard. As we roared away, we heard a pistol shot ring through the air, undoubtedly a gesture to emphasize the fact that we were unwelcome guests at Little Aspen on the Eastern Slope. I was glad that we were on a down-grade so that our departure was a rapid one. Hank was a skillful driver, and he was angry, so it didn't take us long to get back to the main road.

Hank was silent for quite some time as we continued our somewhat perilous rapid descent. I finally broke the silence.

"That's the place we went camping, I'm sure. I recognized the outline of Jones Peak shortly before we were stopped. They sure are tearing the place up, judging from the dust and the sound of earthmovers."

This seemed to rouse Hank from his private thoughts.

"It's obvious that the operation bears looking into from the standpoint of the legality of what they're doing. That might get at the VonBronigan interests, though I doubt if they could be stopped. But that doesn't really give us a lever on Bob Wexler, unless of course he has some financial involvement in the project. That would be hard to track down, though. The Bauer legal experts are very clever at obfuscating the workings of their client's businesses. And between the VonBronigans and the Bauer outfit, things will be so involved that it would take us months to get the tangle sorted out so it could be exposed. By then the election will be over. Bob may be clean anyway. But it's something to think about. I intend to get at the swine sooner or later, but there's so much money and power to fight! It's a real challenge, that's for sure!"

The remainder of the trip down to Denver was marked by sporadic conversation. Hank would lapse into long silences, and it was obvious that he was thinking about the problems he was facing. I made occasional remarks about the scenery or the traffic or whatever small talk I could dredge up, but the usually affable and in-control-of-things Hank Davis was obviously suffering from his defeat on the slopes of Jones Peak. I found my own spirits considerably dampened by Hanks' change of mood. And the brief skirmish at Jones Peak hadn't made me feel all that great either. I had to fight off a feeling of total inadequacy to cope with the situation. All the while my more sane, objective self kept saying, "But you are inadequate, you know!"

Nor was I reassured by Hank's remarks as we got into downtown Denver.

"I'll let you off on Twentieth Street. You'll have to walk to your place. I don't want to be seen letting you out in front of the VonBronigan's building. And we had best not communicate by phone from your place either. They might just decide to tap the phone, in case they get at all suspicious of you. In a couple of days call me at my office or at home in the evening. Use a pay phone to let me know what's developing. And do be careful. These people play for keeps, you know."

Having seen the big bruiser at the gate on Jones Peak, I didn't need to be told that. I thanked Hank for the lunch and for the afternoon's excitement, and he drove away, lost immediately in the late afternoon traffic of downtown Denver.

Oswald G. Ragatz

    I spent an hour and a half strolling back toward my apartment. It was interesting to see the changes in this part of the city that had taken place during the past twenty-five years. The tower that had stood at the corner of the old Daniels and Fishers department store was still there, though the store itself had been torn down. But the tower looked pretty forlorn. I remembered how exciting it had been when as a kid my parents had taken me up to the observation deck during a brief visit to Denver. Now declared an historic landmark, the tower was dwarfed by the nearby skyscrapers erected during the oil boom years. The slender tower looked quite out of place now, and for a moment I had this strange feeling of empathy for the old structure. We both were out of step with our surroundings and were having difficulty justifying our being here. The tower was an "historic landmark", but what was I? Neither historic nor a landmark, but maybe I was about to become just a mark, a target for some thug sharpshooter employed by the VonBronigans. I shuddered and actually looked behind me, which was utterly ridiculous, since I hadn't done anything to jeopardize my standing with that unsavory bunch, not yet anyway. I ducked into a small restaurant where I ate an indifferent supper.

    Another hour's stroll about the Larimer Square area calmed me down, and by the time I'd returned to my fancy abode, I was in a sane enough state of mind to call Lucille. She was still at her mother's, but she would have to return home by next Monday for the start of the summer term at the University. Our conversation was general. Since we had always been very open with each other, I felt a bit guilty about it, but I just couldn't explain what I was really up to, here in Denver. She thought I was just helping an old friend with a political campaign and making some good money during the summer months. I'd just let it go at that. Anyway, nothing would be helped by having her worry. That morning I had called my Dean and had gotten his approval to have my class be taught by my younger colleague. The Dean would take care of the arrangements.

After watching television for some time, I went up to my bedroom on the upper level and then out on the terrace where I could look down over the imposing cityscape. It was a beautiful scene, enhanced by a nearly full moon which actually made it possible to see a dark outline of the mountains to the west. But a great loneliness overcame me. This was certainly not the ambience to be experienced alone. This was almost immediately followed by a great sense of foreboding danger, and I quickly turned and went back into my bedroom and after a quick shower, was in bed. Sleep didn't come easily. I had nothing to read, and there were too many thoughts jostling for attention in my mind. Finally, however, I fell into an uneasy slumber, disturbed by dreams involving a great expanse of snow being cleared away by bulldozers driven by men in plaid shirts with guns at their side. And Jake Harrell was there, looking twenty-one years old as he had the last time I saw him.

The next three days were uneventful. I spent long hours in the city library going through periodicals and books which might fill me in on Colorado development, politics, history, or anything else that might help me get a handle on the situation. For bedtime reading, I checked out a book, "Silver Dollar", an historical novel dealing with H.A.W.Tabor, legendary silver prospector who hit it rich and who was important in the early days of the city. I also spent a lot of time at the Denver Post where Hank had arranged for me to have a little room in which to peruse back issues of newspapers. A very efficient secretary periodically dropped in to see what I might need and to bring me materials from the morgue. At no time did I see Hank. However, I called him each evening from some pay phone as he had instructed.

I met with Ron Dawson on Thursday morning to help him plan some strategy for Wexler's meeting with a labor group the coming weekend. Bob was flying back from Washington Friday afternoon, and we were to meet with him that night to give him the speech to be delivered Saturday night to a group from the truckers union. Ron was less ineffectual when he was not in the presence of the VonBronigans. He actually was a rather pleasant chap, intelligent, low key, and easy to work with. I began to have the feeling that he was as uncomfortable in his position as I was. He had a wife and four kids, and I figured that he had taken the job as Bob's campaign manager out of financial necessity rather than out of commitment to the Wexler campaign as such. He'd been messing about in local politics most of his life, so he knew a lot of the ins and outs of the Denver and Colorado political scenes, which I found helpful. He was no intellectual heavy, though, and he displayed considerable deference to me when I made suggestions. I was glad that he didn't seem to resent this intrusion of an egg-head into his arena.

When I got back to my pad Thursday evening after a light supper in a little restaurant near by, I found the light blinking on the answering machine. It was Jessamin wanting me to call her, so I dialed the Wexler number. The Chicano girl answered the phone, but in a moment Jessamin's seductive voice was purring at me. I couldn't help but wonder if the feline claws were completely withdrawn, however. There was something in her voice that made me uneasy.

"Don, you must be exhausted from all your library work this week. Ron Dawson told me about your meeting with him this morning. He said you had some fine suggestions, and that you seemed to already know more about Colorado than we natives do."

I must admit that I was pleased as I replied, "Well, I'm trying to do my job."

"Well, don't overdo the work, Don. All work and no play makes a dull boy, you know.!" If ever I had heard an invitation to "play", this was it. But I wasn't falling for that old line.

"Don't worry. I'm used to library work and lots of reading."

When she spoke again, Jessamin's voice changed character entirely. She was now the no-nonsense, let's-get-it-out-on-the-table VonBronigan heiress.

"By the way, I had a chat with Uncle Karl. He said that the guard up at that resort development had reported that a couple of men had been snooping around earlier in the week. He got the license plate of their car and had it looked up. It belongs to Henry Davis, the editor at the Denver Post who is out after Bob's hide. We're curious as to how he had gotten wind of the Jones Peak development. All the people working up there are VonBronigan men, and they're pretty trustworthy. That is, they know which side of their bread their butter is on. Davis is married to one of your and Bob's old classmates. Well, actually, Bob's first wife, as you no doubt know. By any chance, you haven't seen either of the Davises since our meeting Sunday, have you? We thought you might have mentioned something about the development, since we talked about it quite a bit at dinner Sunday evening."

I was horrified! I am not accustomed to lying. As a matter of fact, I am not accustomed to finding myself in a position where I need to lie. But I couldn't—what do they call it?—blow my cover at this point. I hoped Jessamin didn't notice how long it took me to reply.

"I saw them at the reunion, of course. Amanda introduced me to her husband. But nothing was said, nothing could have been said, about the development on Jones Peak. Surely with all the activity that must be going on up there, it would be pretty hard to keep it a secret."

Of course, I knew there was a lot of activity going on on the slopes of Jones Peak. There had been an awful lot of dust in the air. Now I just hoped that during the Sunday evening conversation there had been some mention of such activity. I'd just now almost given away the fact that I knew something about the project, more than I should know.

Jessamin seemed satisfied with my reply, but I still had an uneasy feeling. It was guilt, no doubt. As I said, I'm not used to lying.

"Well, we just don't want that project to muck up Bob's campaign. We tried to get Uncle Karl to wait until after election, but he is such a stubborn old fart. When he decides to do something, there is absolutely no stopping him. I sometimes think he doesn't give a damn about getting Bob elected. That is, until he thinks of the advantages, past and future, of having a member of the family in the Senate."

As I spoke again, I felt like some poor, scared dog crawling on its stomach, rolling big, sad eyes, slowly wagging a dispirited tail, as a possible aggressor, stick in hand, approaches.

"Oh, I do understand. I do understand. We will have to watch the press for any signs that an issue is going to be made of the Jones Peak situation. I'll talk to Bob this weekend, and to Ron Dawson, and see if we can have a contingency maneuver waiting, just in case anything does come out."

"That will be a very good idea." Jessamin's voiced sounded remote and a bit hard. I had the feeling that she had sensed that I had not been forthcoming. She was one sharp cookie, and hard as nails. I shuddered as I contemplated the fact that I was up against the VonBronigan amoral ruthlessness plus Bob Wexler's amoral ambitions. I hoped that my voice wasn't shaking as I forced myself to reply.

"I'll be looking forward to seeing you soon, probably tomorrow evening. Ron said that he and I were to meet with Bob at your place in the evening to get things set up for that Saturday night meeting with the labor group."

Suddenly Jessamin was all seductive and feminine.

"Oh, I'll be looking forward to seeing you too, though you will be busy with Bob. Let's arrange some time when we don't have to think about politics or business. Let's aim for some afternoon early next week, here at the house by the pool, just the two of us. I'd love to get to know you better. We can have a cool swim if it's hot—and I think it's supposed to be hot next week. Don't bother about rounding up a suit, though. We can just skinny dip. The servants are very discrete. Till then, bye-bye you old sobersides political scientist." She hung up.

I was aghast. And impressed. This woman could change moods faster than turning on or off a light switch. Her last sentence had been delivered with seductive mockery, obviously with the intent of making me rise to the bait. I couldn't believe what had been happening to me this past week. Had it only been a week? It seemed impossible! I couldn't remember when, if ever, any woman had come on to me like Marilou had and now Jessamin! At DeMott University I was, indeed, just that rather dull, sobersides political science professor, devoted father and faithful husband, unassailable, and not worth the effort anyway. I sat for some time before I realized I was still holding the phone in my hand. I slowly put it on its cradle, and somehow this routine action brought some reason to my bemused mind. I needn't think that Jessamin was all that enthralled with "getting to know me better" because I was such a desirable hunk. She didn't do anything that wasn't calculated to be to her benefit. No doubt "getting to know me better" was part of some much bigger picture, possibly to get me in a situation where I'd divulge my connection with Hank Davis, for instance. As for Marilou, well, that had been just getting some old disappointments, frustrations, and guilts taken care of, only a little interlude before her publisher lover Bert arrived for his summer month in that lovenest in the mountains. I knew all this, but I had to admit that it was sort of fun to be experiencing this pretense of being some Don Juan pursued by these beautiful women.

I wandered up to the terrace. There was a heavy smog over the city. This night there was no seeing the mountains to the west in the moonlight! The lights on the streets below were not clear, and I decided that the smog must have permeated my brain. I thought over Jessamin's conversation and realized that instead of reacting like some silly teenager about to be introduced to the mysteries of sex, I'd better be thinking about my hide! Could that brute guard at the gate of Little Aspen on the Eastern Slope have been able to describe me so that the VonBronigans would know I was the one with Hank? For a minute I seriously considered taking the next plane out of Denver.

A new thought came to me. I realized I had been counting on Hank Davis's being omnipotent. Nothing could possibly happen to me with Hank at the helm. But now I realized that

Hank, too, was human. Here he had me being so careful about phone calls and not being seen with him, but he had used his own car to drive the two of us up to Jones Peak! In a way, it was comforting to know that even Hank Davis was human. In another way, it was terrifying to realize that he could make mistakes, big mistakes, and that I might suffer because of his errors. Suffer! Good God, be killed was more like it. Yes, these people played for keeps!

A hot shower and two aspirin helped me finally to get to sleep, but it was not an easy sleep. I felt groggy all day Friday, but I slogged away at Bob's speech, and I met Ron late in the afternoon to put on some final touches. The Senator would get into Denver about dinner-time and would need to have time to get from the airport, get cleaned up, and eat. This gave Ron and me time for a reasonably quiet dinner together at some place downtown, then we drove out to Wexler's. This time, I might add, I did not get lost.

CHAPTER 12

When we got to the Wexlers, the oriental fellow led us into the library. There was no sign of Jessamin. Bob came in a minute later as Ron was laying out the double-spaced cards with the speech typed in capital letters. After we had all sat down at the table, Bob read over the speech, making no comment. Then he looked up, focusing his eyes on some point between Ron and me.

"You've done a good job, boys. This ought to convince the bastards to support me."

I found his derogatory term in reference to his constituency offensive, but, of course, I said nothing. I hoped I dissembled. Naturally, I was relieved that he liked the speech which Ron and I had put together. We had worked pretty hard to effectively skirt any real issues that might cause problems with this particular group. I was despising the whole process, but I kept reminding myself of the real reason I was there.

Bob was quiet for a minute or two, and he looked worried or displeased, I couldn't tell which. He was not his usual confident, ebullient self, that was sure. I thought maybe he was just tired from his trip west. But it wasn't to be that simple.

"I have a new problem we need to worry about. Well, really, two problems." Bob leaned forward, putting his elbows on the table at which we were seated and his finger tips together under his chin. He didn't look at either Ron or me. He just focused on that far-away spot between the two of us as he began to speak. His voice was hard.

"Someone is out to get me, and I think I know who it is. Uncle Karl called me in Washington on Wednesday. He had had a report from the watchman at that development on Jones Peak. A couple of guys were snooping around up there Monday, and when the license plate was traced, it turned out that the car belonged to Henry Davis, that bastard at the Denver Post. I wouldn't take that too seriously if there wasn't something else that came up while I was in Washington. I found out that some guy has been making inquiries and talking to some former employees of mine in my office there. I'm pretty sure it's a fellow that used to work with Davis on the Washington Post. The son-of-a-bitch is now a private investigator, a very good one, I understand. I can't see that he would have any interest in me unless someone here in Denver had hired him. And that points to Davis. Of course, you know that bitch that Davis is married to was my first wife, so they have a personal grudge as well as a political grudge. Davis is one of these goddamn do-gooders, all cozy-wozy with the environmentalists and all that fuckin' crowd. And he's dangerous! I can't afford to have the Post come out with any real damaging facts. Their innuendos we can cope with, but I'd hate to have Davis dig up anything really specific to hit me with."

I tried to look as ingenuous as possible.

"How did you find out about this private eye?"

Bob looked at me, the first time our eyes had actually met.

He spoke through clenched teeth.

"That is not relevant. I just know how to make the most of people's inability to keep their mouths shut, especially women."

I let that pass, but I figured that his ex-secretary had probably said something to someone, and that someone had gotten back to the Senator. I tried to look worried—well, concerned at least. I wished I'd taken some courses in drama when in college.

"But what could they possibly come up with something that could be so damaging?"

Bob's eyes focused on that far-away spot again, and he didn't answer for some time. He seemed to be having difficulty formulating an answer to my question. Finally his eyes swiveled to mine, and his expression seemed to be one of hostile challenge. I think I actually felt a cold chill run up my back. Then he spoke.

"When my second wife killed herself—I assume you know about that—I happened to have gone to New York that afternoon. I didn't tell my office why I was going. It was none of their goddamn business. Actually, I had a date with this woman that sometimes, ah, helps me to relieve the tensions of my office. My wife Tillie was a dud in the sack, and anyway she was here in Denver. It wasn't 'till the next afternoon when I got back to Washington that I got the word that Tillie had connected a hose to the exhaust of her car and had conked out. I presumed she had found out about my friend in New York, and as a matter of fact, the local gossip at the time rather fancied that sort of explanation. But there was never anything in the press indicating that the Senator from Colorado was anything but a faithful family man, devastated by the death of his ever-loving wife. Connections help, you know. And I've assumed that people have forgotten about it. Voters have very short memories."

During Bob's speech of self-justification, I'd gotten myself under control and was able to play along with the charade. Trying to look every bit the man of the world and very sympathetic, I asked.

"So what's the big deal, especially if it's been forgotten? You're hardly the first congressman to—how'd you put it—have someone other than a wife help relieve the tensions of office. Didn't Thomas Jefferson set the precedent?"

I couldn't believe what I was saying. What an immoral bastard I'd become. But Bob didn't seem to be reassured by my assumed worldly nonchalance.

"O.K. That's true. But just suppose that someone comes up with, I mean fabricates, some tale about my flying from New York to Denver that night. Just the suggestion that I had engineered Tillie's suicide could ruin me, no matter whether it was true or not. And right now the climate across the country is to discredit the legislators by digging up some little episode in the past which is considered naughty. Think what the press would do with a suggestion of murder!"

I thought maybe I should open my eyes in disbelief, though I have a hunch I was already pretty pop-eyed!

"But whoever dreamed up such a scenario would have to have SOME proof of such a tale, and if you hadn't...."

Bob interrupted me.

"But that's just what worries me. I happen to know that this snoop has already tracked me to New York—no problem. BUT suppose he, ah, somehow claims to have found a record of my flying to Denver, whether I did or not is beside the point."

Bob's expression of alarm turned to one of veiled caution.

He seemed to have realized that he might have given himself away with his remarks—like "whether it was true or not" and "whether I did or not...." I wondered what facial muscles I should use to look ingenuous.

"I don't see why you're so worried, Bob. If someone does launch this sort of smear campaign, I think Ron and I can come up with some way to diffuse it."

Ron Dawson had not said a word through all this, and as I made this last statement, I looked at him. For just an instant I was sure I caught a look of complete cynicism on his face. Then he dissembled beautifully as he nodded assent. I decided then and there that our Mr. Dawson could give me a lesson or two in the fine art of hiding one's thoughts and emotions. Unfortunately, at that instant, my wife's remarks about my mobile features flashed through my mind. No reassurance from that quarter!

Bob stood up, pulled in his rib cage and threw back his padded shoulders.

"I'm tired, boys, and I have to read over these pearls of wisdom you have put together for me. The meeting tomorrow night is at seven-thirty. We should get there a half hour beforehand, to shake hands and kiss the asses of the big-shot labor leaders who'll be there in full cry. I'll see you boys at the hall. And thanks for the good job on this oration."

As Bob showed us to the door, I was pondering his use of the words 'pearls of wisdom' and 'oration.' Had there been some hint of sarcasm? But I decided that he probably was just being ironic, sort of letting us know that he knew that we knew what a sham all this was. This implied acceptance of my being a part of the inner circle in the collusion and deception added to my feeling of discomfort with the whole situation.

We had driven at least a couple of miles before either Ron or I said anything. Then with a great sigh, Ron broke the silence.

"This is the last one of these jobs I'm going to take...if we survive this one. I've applied for a position dealing with public relations for a company in Cheyenne. If I get the job, I'm taking my family out of here as fast as possible. No more of this miserable political crap."

This prompted me to ask, "Do you think there really might be something to the Senator's concern? I mean, could he actually have been in Denver the night his wife committed suicide?"

We drove several blocks before Ron answered.

"It is not for me to express an opinion. My job is to present the Senator to the public in such a way as to insure his election. I'm paid well to do so. I've a family to support and kids to get through college. As long as I am being paid to do this job, I have no personal opinions. I assume that your position is the same as mine, though I've not figured out why you find it necessary to be here when you have a good job teaching back at your university. At first I assumed it was because of a long time friendship with the Senator, but somehow I don't sense that there really is a basic loyalty between you two."

This was an invitation to state my own feelings about the situation, but I wasn't about to risk my safety by letting anyone know what I was really up to. How did I know that Ron wasn't just pumping me on the behest of Bob Wexler? Anyway, I was only half listening to Ron. My mind finally was coming to grips with the fact that Hank's carelessness in using his car for the trip to Jones Peak had alerted Bob to the fact that something was afoot. Somehow, when Jessamin had aprised me of the fact that our visit had been reported, I'd not realized how much danger might be involved. And could that goon at the gate identify me as the other man with Hank? If he could, then the whole project of nailing Wexler with a murder charge would be blown sky high. And I'd be blown sky high with it. Possibly literally! I think Ron was still talking, but I hadn't the slightest idea of what he was saying. I was engulfed in a great wave of total fear. I knew that I had to let Hank Davis know about this new development, and I found myself driving well over the speed limit. Fortunately, no police saw me. The rest of the trip into downtown Denver was made in silence. I let Ron off at a garage where he had parked his car, and after shaking hands, we went our independent ways, each pondering thoughts at which the other could only guess.

I parked my car in the basement garage of my building, but I did not go up to the apartment. I went out a side door and walked to a drug store a few blocks away where there was a public phone booth. My hand was shaking as I put the coins in the slot. Hank answered immediately, but his voice sounded sleepy. It was only then that I realized that it was past midnight.

I was probably a bit incoherent as I told Hank about Wexler's remarks. Hank's reply echoed my own distress.

"My God, what a fool I was to use my own car, though I had no idea there was going to be a guard posted! But I should have known that the VonBronigans would do just that! How could I have been such a fool?"

If I'd been more in control of myself, I'd never have answered this rhetorical question. As it was, I blurted out, "Yea, I wondered about that." Then realizing what I'd just said, I started to make amends. But Hank interrupted.

"Of course you did. And you have every right to. I've been instrumental in getting you involved in this mess, and while I don't see how he could do it, if Wexler finds out you were the man with me, you are, as one of our recent presidents said, in deep doo-doo."

That Hank had not taken offence once again proved his class.

He may have made a big blunder, but he was a real top-drawer guy.

For a moment I was tempted to forgive him for the blunder, but then my mouth seemed ahead of my mind as I heard myself replying.

"Yea, deep doo doo, like being the next victim of that bastard's murdering mind! He was strange tonight. Well, not strange, but I saw a side of him that has not been obvious before. Anger, even fear, and a steely resolve to find out all the details. He's obviously got a network of informants in Washington. It's my guess that before many more days pass he will know about your efforts to get information about his flight to Denver on the night Tillie died."

I was not sure that Hank was listening to me, though I'd discovered that he had the kind of mind that was capable of operating efficiently on two levels at the same time. At any rate, his next remark indicated that he was already figuring out ways to counter the new developments.

"Here's what I am going to do for now. I believe you said that there is to be a big meeting of labor groups tomorrow night to hear the Senator tell the downtrodden how much he loves them. Instead of sending a regular reporter to cover the meeting, I'll send one of my confidants, and the story he will write for the Sunday morning edition will be a complimentary and glowing report of the Senator's speech. There will be no innuendos or implied attacks on his platform. Then Monday, since the VonBronigans know it was I who went to Jones Peak, there will be a story saying that I had hoped to see what progress was being made on the great VonBronigan developments on Jones Peak. This will baffle our readers, but we have to throw the VonBronigans and Wexler off the scent for a while. I doubt that it will fool them for very long, but it may throw them off balance, long enough for us to bring this all to a head. We will come clean with the readers when we expose Wexler for what he is. Do you have anything new that could back up our suspicions of murder?"

Oswald G. Ragatz

I told Hank about my impression that Wexler had twice used words that suggested that he had indeed flown to Denver from New York the night Tillie died. But that was only a hunch, an impression on my part. Of course, there had been absolutely nothing that would implicate Bob in engineering Jake Harrell's death on the slopes of the Jones Peak glacier. At no time had Jake even been mentioned in my various conversations with Bob. We had talked almost exclusively about the campaign, speeches and concomitant matters. As for Hank's proposed planted stories in the Post, I wasn't particularly reassured. As I thought about it, the maneuver might further implicate me. Only Ron and I knew of the 'new developments' that Bob had reported to us. If Bob saw the news stories for what they really were—a subterfuge—it would not take much imagination to figure out where the information had come from that had prompted the seeming change in the policy of the Denver Post. It would be logical to connect Donald Moffett with "The Old Gang," namely Marilou Baxter and Amanda Forsythe, now Mrs. Hank Davis, and ergo, Hank Davis himself. I tried to reassure myself that the Senator from Colorado wasn't too bright. I'd always known that, and the fact that he had hired me had proven the point. This smug idea was terminated almost immediately by my rational self pointing out that I'd certainly not been very bright myself to take the job. What was the cliché? "Putting one's head in the noose," I thought it was. I was just beginning to wonder if Hank realized what a dangerous spot this all put me when he interrupted my thoughts.

"You realize that you are in real danger. Don't put yourself into a situation where you are alone with Wexler. It's no telling what he might try if he finds out that you're a mole. That whole clan is ruthless, and from what you and the girls have told me, Bob Wexler is the most lethal of them all."

I'm sure my voice whined, plaintively maybe. "So what do I do now? I'd like to go back home to Jeffreysville!" .

Hank's reply was firm though hardly reassuring.

Reunion With Murder

"You would be no safer in Jeffreysville than in Denver. People with dangerous information are tracked down wherever they are. No, what we HAVE GOT to do is finish this thing off and put Senator Wexler behind bars, and fast!"

I excused the slip in Hank's usual impeccable use of the English language. His "have got" certainly did add emphasis to what he was saying. Unaware of my didactic thoughts, he continued.

"For the time being, just go along with what you've been doing. Write him great speeches, though let's hope there will be little opportunity for many more of them. Be the brown-nose sycophant, and for God's, sake keep that mobile face of yours blank!"

I thought I might burst into tears. Telling me to keep my face in repose was like telling Michael Jackson to keep on looking like a Jets linebacker. Nature, or heredity, or DNA or whatever had given me an expressive face. It had a life of its own, motivated by whatever part of the brain controls emotions but bypassing the part of the mind that controls rational behavior. But I knew Hank was right. I had to go on—no turning back now, come what may.

For a moment I wanted to say that I wanted to be in Hanks' protection around the clock, but then I remembered that we were in trouble because Hank hadn't been infallible—had really goofed. I couldn't even depend on him. I was on my own. No more counting on someone else running the defense. I was out there on the thirty-yard line, the pass was coming my way, and I either catch it and run for the touch-down or I get smashed by the VonBronigan team. I mean, smashed dead! I'm not a great football fan, but at the moment this rather brutal sport seemed to epitomize my own situation.

Hank's telling me to keep in touch was like telling a drowning man to continue calling for help. He needn't have bothered with this bit of sage advice. Believe me, I fully intended to keep in touch—as long as I could get to a phone, that is! Of course, corpses can't keep in touch, as no doubt Jake and

Tillie, wherever they are, had discovered. Hank said good-bye and hung up the phone. I can't remember whether or not I even replied. I almost staggered out of the phone booth, through the drug store, and into the street.

I'm not one to resort to alcohol to help me get through a crisis. I actually have considerable contempt for people who do. But now the neon lights of a bar a half block away seemed to offer some momentary relief from my anxiety. In a few moments, I was settling myself at the dimly lit bar and ordering a scotch on the rocks. I was too preoccupied with my thoughts to pay much attention to the surroundings and to the people occupying the various booths along the walls.

CHAPTER 13

The bartender had just served me my scotch on the rocks when I was startled to hear a familiar voice purring in my ear.

"Well, if it isn't Donald Moffett! This IS a surprise!" I almost spilled my drink as I turned to see who it was speaking to me. I knew I should recognize the voice, but until I looked at Larry VonBronigan, it hadn't registered who it was. As I now observed him more closely, it occurred to me for the first time that perhaps he and Jessamin were twins. But contemplation of Larry's physical characteristics was terminated by the necessity of concentrating on what he was saying. His speech was slightly slurred, indicating that he had been partaking of the bartender's libations for quite some time.

"I had no idea that you swung—swang—whatever—both ways. Now I understand why dear sister perhaps hasn't been able to make time with you. She's quite put out about that, you know. Maybe I won't be so unfortunate, yes?"

I was absolutely aghast at these remarks! As the significance of what Larry was saying sank into my already addled brain, I for the first time looked around the room. It was immediately apparent that the couples in the booths or in concentrated conversation at the bar all were male, mostly yuppie age, and all unusually well groomed albeit a bit flashily. It finally dawned on me that I had wandered into a gay bar, and that at this time of night it could safely be assumed by one and all (including Larry, of course) that anyone who was here was here for only one purpose. Larry must have seen my eyes swivel as I had surveyed the scene. He leaned close to me, putting his hand on my arm.

"Nice place here, isn't it? Or were you just looking for someone more desirable? I don't think you should bother, dear boy. I really am quite what anyone could want. I'm terribly glad you came in. I've been here quite a while, but everyone seemed to already be, ah, occupied. I'd about decided that the remainder of the night might have to be spent in an empty bed, a situation which I simply, SIMPLY loathe!"

I hadn't the slightest idea how to get out of the dilemma. Dull political science professors are not accustomed to being propositioned by rich, yuppie gays—at least not those academicians who have sense enough not to wander inadvertently into gay bars. My first impulse was to blurt out a vigorous disclaimer of my sexual preference and of my lack of intentions, but Larry seemed to be taking no chances of this fish getting of the hook. His hand on my arm kept stroking ever so slightly as he sat down on the stool beside me.

"You may not know it, but I've been watching you ever since that Sunday afternoon when the clan convened at Wexler's. That little episode of my nude swimming, which so annoyed my dear sister, was hopefully for your benefit. Actually, I've always been fascinated by my sister's expertise in the matter of establishing liaisons. I've learned a lot from watching her. She's usually successful, too. She's not known as Platte Valley Pussy for nothing! So I've been quite interested and a bit amused that she doesn't seem to be getting anywhere with you. I'd decided that your great devotion to your old friend, my brother-in-law, had kept you from moving in on his wife. But now I understand. Oh, there's an empty booth over there! Let's move over where we can get acquainted. Finish your drink and let me buy you another."

I'd not been aware that I'd been working on my scotch, but now I realized that my glass was nearly empty. I obeyed Larry, and having taken the last swallow of the drink, I found myself being propelled by him to a booth just vacated by two men who were somewhat unsteadily leaving the bar, arm in arm.

Larry continued talking before we got settled in the booth.

"You know, you really don't have to be loyal to Bob Wexler on that score! He makes no pretense of being loyal to his beautiful wife, and as matter of fact, he has quite a soft spot in that black heart of his for his brother-in-law. I do believe that on those occasions when he's in Denver, he has a difficult time deciding whether to bed his lovely wife or the lovely Larry. Oh, let me rephrase that; he has a hard spot in his crotch for his brother-in-law, the lovely Larry."

This candid confession was interrupted by the arrival of fresh drinks. The bartender had gotten some signaled message from Larry as we were leaving for the booth. I didn't have the presence of mind to think about dissembling. I am sure that my face showed fright, amazement, embarrassment—just name all the emotions that go into consuming horror!

I'd not said a word through all this, but Larry didn't seem to expect any rejoinder. He reached across the table and put his hand over mine as he continued.

"I see in those big brown eyes of yours that you still are writing me off as just a bubble-head queer. And actually that pleases me. I mean, it proves that I'm doing what I've set out to do. Dad and Uncle Karl think I haven't the slightest idea of what they are up to most of the time, and my dear brother-in-law is interested in people for only one purpose—to screw them, in bed or at the polls. They're all pretty easy to fool. Now Jessamin is something else. I really have to work at keeping her thinking I am a feckless fop. I was in my teens when it dawned on me that there were tens-of-millions in the VonBronigan Group's portfolio and bank accounts, and I decided then and there that I wanted eventually to have that lovely money just for little old Larry. Oh, don't look disappointed! I use the word little only figuratively. Larry's not little in the areas where it counts!"

I was somewhat encouraged by the fact that Larry was continuing to misinterpret the messages which were undoubtedly being plastered all over my face. However, I by now had had time enough to get my thoughts somewhat under control, and I realized that I had struck a pay lode (isn't what they would have said in this mining state?). Maybe if I could stay sober, if Larry would keep on talking, and if I could eventually get away from him without some disastrous scene, I might have just the information Hank was needing to scuttle the Senator's campaign.

Oswald G. Ragatz

Certainly the information that Senator Wexler was having an affair with his wife's brother could make very interesting front-page news indeed! Though how we could prove that posed a problem.

For a moment, Larry's attention turned to his drink, an approach which involved some pretty impressive gulps, not careful sipping!

This gave me a chance to begin what I hoped would be clever, subtle probing.

"Well, actually, Bob Wexler and I aren't particularly close friends. We once were close twenty-five years ago, but we'd had no contact since then till we came to our twenty-fifth class reunion a week ago. Bob read my bio in the class brochure, and he decided that I might have the expertise he needed to sell his campaign to a restless constituency. He is paying me well, and I might add that a professor's salary is peanuts compared to what the VonBronigans and Wexlers take for granted. I'm approaching my work here as a professional should. I've always made it a point not to become involved sexually with students or colleagues. You know, one shouldn't mix business and pleasure."

I did not add that at the moment I could not think of any occasion when either a student or a colleague had offered me the opportunity to become involved in a liaison. I was pretty sure that the general perception in Jeffreysville and on the DeMott campus was that Prof. Moffett was a pretty stuffy square, best ignored unless in an academic situation.

Larry looked at me in mock pity.

"Tsk, tsk, you must miss out on a lot of fun. I hate to see anyone waste their life with undue caution like that. I'd like to spice things up a bit for you, unless you consider me off limits because of your devotion to your job with the honorable Senator. Why don't you just consider me as someone you've never met before, and let's go on from there?"

This was definitely NOT how I wanted the conversation to go! So trying to match Larry's inflections which gave most of his words the effect of suggestive innuendo, I hastily replied.

"Oh, I don't think that's a problem. *Au contraire.* You aren't in anyway my employer."

And then, having decided on a *modus operandi,* I went one dangerous step further.

"I must admit that I have been very attracted to Jessamin. She is what I might call a 'dish', or is that term passé? And you resemble her a great deal. You both have those marvelous green eyes."

I almost choked on this. That was as close as I could come to saying that Larry had beautiful green eyes and that I found him attractive. I was suddenly infused with terror at the thought that maybe I really did find him attractive. But I couldn't take time-out to contemplate my buried id, so I rushed on.

"The first time I met your sister at the reunion banquet, I couldn't keep my eyes off her lovely features."

I didn't add that actually the most arresting features which had tempted my eyes had been a couple of outstanding items somewhat below the neck line, bravely holding up that skin-tight dress she had worn. At the moment, that wasn't the image I wanted to establish in this crazy charade in which I was becoming embroiled.

This talk about green eyes made Larry, consciously or unconsciously, bat his eyelids in a disgusting, exaggerated flutter.

I tried hard not to look revolted. For the moment, my id was reassured—or was I reassured in spite of my id—or...?

Larry took over the conversation while I continued my uncomfortable self-questioning.

"Well, thank you, dear boy. I'm glad we understand each other."

I cringed inwardly as he continued, rather recklessly I thought. He obviously had imbibed too much alcohol, and the tongue was loosened. So much the better for my half-baked plan.

"Now don't think I don't enjoy the little encounters of the sweet kind with my brother-in-law. But he really is a bastard, and I'm not fooled for a minute about his dirty intentions. Both he and my dear sister want to get me into a position with the old men where they will disinherit me. Sometime I'm afraid I've played the quixotic-queer bit too successfully. Not that they care particularly about my sex life; they're a little beyond that. But the prospect of their hard-won—note, I did not say hard-earned—lucre falling into inept hands can well do me in. I'm considering doing some big reform act to convince the old boys that I'd be a competent heir. But what really worries me is my dear brother-in-law. I'm sure that when Jessamin inherits, all or half, he will have some nefarious scheme to get rid of her so that he can get his filthy paws on all that money. Now I don't have a lot of love for my sister, but I don't wish her an end like that of Tillie Wexler. Actually, I'd be content with just half the estate and let Jessamin have her half, IF Bob Wexler wasn't going to share it with her or inherit all of her share!"

Larry finished off his drink, which gave me a chance to pickup on his last remarks.

"Do you really think Jessamin would kill herself over something her husband did?"

Larry's eyes widened.

"Who said anything about her killing herself? Nothing Bob Wexler could do would make her be so stupid. I meant, HE'D devise some way to get her laid out in the family crypt!"

Larry signaled the bartender for more drinks while I attempted to looked shocked and surprised.

"You can't really mean that Bob might resort to murder!"

Taking a long swallow of the fresh drink, he then leaned across the table. His hand tightened on mine.

"Listen carefully to me, my dear professor, and I'll clue you in on life of the rich and famous as I observe it from a front-row seat. Now I can't prove this, but I DON'T think the last Mrs.

Wexler killed herself. I knew Tillie Bauer pretty well. I've always had lots of friends who are involved in the arts, and when she came back from Europe and started spreading some of the Bauer money around, I saw quite a bit of her. When she married the up-and-coming lawyer, Robert Wexler, we all figured that it was just a ploy on his part. Tillie was a nice person, but somewhat of a dog, hardly the sort that a handsome guy like Wexler would divorce an attractive wife like Amanda for. At first, Tillie was ecstatically in love. I think she'd given up any hope of ever landing a husband. She was quite a bit older than Wexler, too, which made it all the more improbable. But it wasn't long before she began to see that she'd been used to get Wexler established in her father's law firm. Incidentally, that's where the VonBronigans first became aware of the Wexler talents."

I was afraid that Larry was going to go off in another direction in his conversation. His speech was becoming more and more slurred, and he seemed to be having some difficulty concentrating on what he was saying. I decided to steer him back to the subject of Tillie. Nothing he had said so far was news to me, but I very badly wanted to know why he didn't think Tillie had killed herself.

"You said that you didn't think Tillie killed herself. I should have thought that Bob's penchant for philandering would have been motive enough for a wife to commit suicide, since you say that she had doted on her husband."

Larry snorted, spray of his last mouthful of drink nearly hitting me in the face. He was getting disgustingly drunk, but he still could communicate very well.

"No way, José, not Tillie. By the time her husband had gone to Washington, she knew what the score was. She had a lot of friends an' was makin' an interestin' life for herself. She had actually gone back to sculpturin' and was doin' some pretty good work. Shortly before she died she'd had a successful exhibit of some of her things at the Denver Art Museum. And she'd begun to write and had just finished writin' a play which was going to

Oswald G. Ragatz

be put on by the Denver Civic Theater group. I had lunch with her and a couple of friends two days before she died, and she was up-beat and excited about how her life was goin'. Someone tactlessly asked her what her husband thought about her successes, and she just laughed and said something like 'I don't care what th' bastard thinks; he's nothin' to me.' Now that was no woman mournin' for the loss of a husband's love!"

Now was the time for the crucial question. And it had to be asked pretty quickly because Larry was showing evidence of becoming what one might call an unreliable witness.

"So how do you think her death was managed? I mean, wasn't the Senator in Washington?"

Larry seemed to be having difficulty focusing on my face. He had removed his hand from the top of mine and now was actually steadying himself on the edge of the table. But his mind was still functioning.

"I don't know how the bastard managed it, but I'm sure he did. Maybe he got someone to get Tillie drunk and then put her in her car and turn on the engine. Maybe he wasn't in Washington. How should I know? I jus' know sweet ol' Tillie di'n't do hershelf in. I gotta go pee."

Larry managed to get himself upright and staggered to the men's room at the back of the room with occasional help of the ends of the booths. I decided I'd gotten all the information from Larry that I could. My next problem was to get out of some nasty confrontation with him over my not going home with him—or to my place which was only a couple of blocks away.

If anyone had told me earlier what I was about to do next, I would have sued them for slander. But desperate situations call for desperate measures. And I felt desperate! Larry's glass was empty again, and the bartender was giving me a high sign that there would be no more serving our table. It was near the 2 o'clock closing time anyway, and the place was almost empty. But my glass was still full. I wasn't about to risk loosing control of myself by drinking any more. The situation was out of control—actually had never been in control ever since that blasted class reunion. I glanced at the bartender, whose back was for a moment toward me, and I emptied my glass into Larry's. I hoped that would be enough to just about knock him out, but that it wouldn't get to him until I got him out of the place and home—his home.

Larry came stumbling back, and after taking a big swig from his glass, he mumbled, "Thatsh better; some relief but not what we'll be 'njoyin' when we get up ta your place."

He reached under the table and gave my knee a squeeze. This had to terminate; I was frantic.

"Larry, let's go now. Finish your drink while I pay the bartender."

This gave me a chance to ask the bartender where we could get a cab. He said I probably could find one at the next corner or maybe one would just be cruising the area. At that point, Larry came reeling over and draped himself on my shoulder.

"Meet my besh' frien', MISHTER Donald Moffitt. He writes speeches fo' the Senator, an' I'm going to give him a BIG blow job an' then we're goin' tuh..."

But I didn't give him a chance for any more graphic discussion of his expectations. I managed to get him out the door, very conscious of the cynical stares of the bartender and a couple of patrons still in a front booth.

For once fate was with me. An empty cab was going by and came to a screeching halt as the result of my shout, "CAB!"

I poured Larry into the back seat and asked him what his address was. His answer told me that he wasn't entirely out of it yet.

"Oh, Donnie boy, lets go tuh your place. I know it's in our building a couple 'v' blocks from here. I don' wanta wait..."

My mind was racing. I'd not gotten in the cab yet, but any idea I had of ditching Larry at this point was dashed by the gruff voice of the driver.

"Look, buster, I aint takin' your drunk pal home by myself. You go along and tuck him in somewhere, not me."

Perjury, more perjury, but I had to think fast. Getting in beside Larry, I took his hand and as convincingly as possible said something to the effect that I'd rather go to his place because he undoubtedly had a larger bed, and anyway there wasn't anything to drink at my place. This seemed to satisfy him, and he gave the driver his address, which turned out to be an apartment on the ground floor of an old sandstone mansion just off Capitol Hill...very posh.

By the time we'd gotten up to Civic Center, Larry was asleep. I felt round in his pockets for some sort of a door key. This aroused him from his stupor, and of course he interpreted it as my making a pass. This prompted him to lean over to try to kiss me. I had just found some keys on a ring, so I pushed him away saying something to the effect that 'not now but later would be better'. He promptly passed out again, and when we got to his pad, he was snoring loudly.

The driver was kind enough to help me get Larry to the door, and he found the right key for me while I kept my drunk charge upright. I tipped the driver handsomely—it was VonBronigan money after all. I'd just gotten my first big check that afternoon and had sent it off to Lucille to bank. Well, the day before actually, since it was well into Saturday by now.

Larry's apartment was very elegant, with much evidence of his devotion to the contemporary arts. Not that I took time to admire his abode. I practically dragged him down a hallway and into what I supposed was his bedroom. There was indeed a king-sized bed, and when I turned on the light, I was greeted by a number of provocative pictures on the walls, all very arty but very erotic. I managed to get Larry undressed and into bed, no small task as he was pretty husky, and I don't have that great an athletic build myself. I didn't bother to straighten out his clothes, which lay about on the floor, and the bed looked pretty disheveled by the time I saw to it that Larry was on his side so that if he got sick, he'd be less apt to choke on his vomit.

I'd not had sense enough to tell the cab driver to wait, and the street was deserted. I walked west a number of blocks down to Broadway, hoping to get an owl car. But I soon realized that owl cars were something remembered from my youth, about like thinking I'd catch the next stage coach. I started to walk north toward Civic Center. When I finally got almost to Sixteenth Street, I was totally exhausted. But just then an empty cab actually did come along and saved my life. Maybe my luck was changing—this was twice in an hour there had been a cab—but I doubted that I could count on my luck's holding out.

It was well past three o'clock when I finally got to my duplex. The night was cold, as so often is the case in Colorado, and the walk had cleared my head of any effects of the two drinks I'd had. I took a long shower and fell into bed. But for all my exhaustion, sleep didn't come quickly, and it was probably nearly four o'clock before my mind stopped rehashing the events, conversations, and impressions of the day...I mean, of the day and of the preceding day.

CHAPTER 14

It was a ringing bell that woke me up, and as I groggily reached for the phone, I could see by my bed clock that it was just one o'clock. The room was flooded with that bright, noonday, Colorado sunlight. It was Ron Dawson on the phone wanting to make arrangements to meet me in front of my building at half past six so that we could get to the hall for the meeting by seven as Bob had wanted.

I felt miserable, but I doubted that I felt half as bad as Larry VonBronigan would, when and if he woke up. A cold shower and a light breakfast helped—I'd gotten in frozen orange juice, instant coffee, and sweet rolls so I could get my own breakfast. I hate going out for breakfast. I could almost hear Larry saying, "I hate, I JUST HATE going out for breakfast." Then I decided he probably had bloody Marys for his breakfast, at least after a night like last night.

After getting dressed, I went down to one of my usual pay-phone booths and tried to contact Hank Davis, but he wasn't available. I left a message that I'd called and would try later. I wasn't ready to start a new project for Bob Wexler, and at that moment, I felt rather at a loss as to what direction we'd be going next. I decided that after this evening's meeting things might become clear again. I was in no mood to work anyway, and on a whim I got my car out of the garage and drove out East Colfax to City Park where the Denver Museum of Natural History offered a diversion.

I'm mildly interested in wild life, and the big dioramas of stuffed animals in their natural habitats were very well done, at least those I could see when they weren't obscured by hoards of children and their shepherding parents. It was a diversion, however, and by the time I got back down town, I was in a pretty good frame of mind. I'd had only my light breakfast, so after I parked my car in the garage, I got an early supper in one of the interesting restaurants in the Larimer Square district. I tried to call Hank at home, but the maid said that they had left for a dinner engagement. It was nearly six when I got back to the apartment, and as I opened the door, I heard the phone ringing. The minute I answered it, I was sorry. It was Larry in full cry.

"Where HAVE you been, you DEAR boy? I've called and called, and I've been just FRANTIC, SIMPLY frantic! When I woke up this morning—well, ACTUALLY this afternoon—and you had left, I was devastated, SIMPLY devastated. Was I good last night? I can't remember a THING after you were making those DELICIOUS passes in the cab. I simply MUST cut holes in my pockets. I HOPE I didn't disappoint you!"

For once I could honestly answer, with no equivocation or dissembling.

"Larry, I assure you that you did not disappoint me in the least. *Au contraire!*"

But I didn't clarify *au contraire* what. Oh, I suppose he might have given me even more information about his unsavory family than he did, but I certainly had gotten a better picture of the dynamics of the VonBronigan Group than I had ever thought I would. I had been congratulating myself all afternoon on how well I had gotten out of the mess with Larry. I had again even allowed myself to hope that getting the two cabs that late at night had been a good omen for the future. But it was too soon for congratulations. As a matter of fact, after another few minutes of Larry's babblings, I realized that this was another problem that wasn't going to go away, and it might become a major one. Larry was his most revolting and manic self.

"Oh! I'm SO glad you enjoyed it. The bedroom AND the bed were SIMPLY a mess when I finally opened my eyes. That's ALWAYS a good sign. And I wouldn't want ANYONE to go away from me frustrated, and especially such a NICE man as you. I just HATE being frustrated myself."

I wondered if my graduation from 'dear boy' to 'nice man' was any improvement in the situation, but I quickly decided to the contrary. I had to answer, so I made with the double talk.

"Larry, you didn't leave me frustrated in the least. Please rest assured." But that wasn't to be the end of it. He gushed on.

"Oh, I'm SO glad. But little old Larry—well, BIG old Larry IS frustrated. Can we get together tonight after that STUPID meeting where my dear brother-in-law will tell all those LIES you and Ron Dawson have written for him?"

I quickly assured Larry that I would be much too tired after the meeting and that no doubt Bob and Ron would want me to talk over the next strategy. I dwelt a bit on how tired I already was, at which point Larry decided to congratulate himself on what a great time he must have given me to make me so tired, and then to chide me for not having stayed the whole night. He began going into a lament that he couldn't remember what we had done the night before and how he just HAD to do something about his drinking too much. I cut in to tell him that I just HAD to go change my clothes so that I'd be ready for Ron when he double parked in front of the building. As I was putting the phone on the cradle, I thought I heard Larry saying that he wished that he was where he could watch me undress. I had never experienced anything like this in my life. Or as Larry would have said, I would NEVER, EVER...my God, I was beginning to think like him or at least talk like him in my head!

Fifteen minutes later, I was getting into Ron's car, still considerably shaken by Larry's phone call. We got to the big hall in plenty of time to huddle with the Senator and go over some minor changes he thought he'd like to make in the speech.

There was a big crowd, mostly working class people, and by no means all men. There was a notable number of dark skinned people, Spanish-Americans, or Mexicans as they were generally called in this area. I felt considerable hostility emanating from the audience as Bob began his talk, but as the minutes wore on and the glib Senator said all the things they wanted to hear, never mind that he didn't mean them, or even know what he was saying half the time, there developed a sense of rapport. By the time it was over, Bob got a big hand, and a lot of people crowded around him to shake his hands. I was consumed with shame.

Many of the things he had said were my own words, and I knew that they weren't worth the ink that would print them in the Sunday edition of the Rocky Mountain News. In the back of the hall, I had seen one well-dressed man taking copious notes, and I had a hunch it was the special reporter from the Denver Post that Hank had sent.

Bob did, indeed, want to talk over what Ron and I were to do next, so we met at a quiet restaurant near downtown and spent a couple of hours over sandwiches and beer. Bob seemed relaxed, buoyed up by what he perceived as his success with the working class. There was none of the tension I had felt in our meeting the night before. He was leaving for Washington on Sunday afternoon and would be back the following Friday night, so we had to get things pretty well outlined before we broke up.

It was nearly midnight when I got back to my duplex and found the light on the answering phone flashing. It was Larry, of course, saying that he'd be home ALONE and I MUST call him the MINUTE I got in. He knew that his mean old brother-in-law was working me MUCH too hard and I simply HAD to take some time off and have some fun. He just HATED to be alone, and he was sure we could have a DELICIOUS evening.

Well, I decided Larry could go to hell, and I called Lucille instead, although it was pretty late. After a long conversation, during which I answered most of her questions with vague generalities, I took a shower and fell into bed. No late night visit to an unknown bar this evening!

It was late Sunday morning when the ringing phone again awakened me. I waited for a few rings, hoping that it would stop, but then I decided that if it were Larry, I'd just tell him what the situation really was. But it wasn't Larry; it was Jessamin purring into the phone. However, the words were almost the same as Larry's.

"You POOR man! I know my husband has been working you MUCH too hard. You need to relax and have some fun. I just HATE being alone. I'm taking Bob to the airport at one o'clock. Can I drop by and pick you up and bring you back here to the house? It's a lovely day and the pool is heavenly warm. I'm sure we could have a DELICIOUS afternoon." Surely these two predatory people must be twins! Again my mouth seemed to be ahead of my thoughts, though this time Mouth said the right things.

"That sounds delightful, but unfortunately my wife is to call me some time between two and four, and if I weren't here, there would be the devil to pay." An out and out lie—well, two lies to be exact, since Lucille never (NEVER) gave me the devil. But somewhere in the back of my mind I'd remembered someone saying that nothing turned off a woman faster than the mention of loyalty to one's wife. And it worked! Jessamin changed instantly from seductress to the hard-edged, matter-of-fact business woman that she really was. But I wasn't happy with the sense of implied threat in her voice.

"Well, you are the careful one! Being too careful can get one in trouble at times, you know. You really don't know what you're missing. We VonBronigans didn't get where we are by being cautious. And as a matter of fact, we prefer people who meet us on our terms. You should know that we also don't appreciate being turned down. Well, if you change your mind, I'm free Tuesday afternoon—and evening for that matter. But don't count on many more opportunities like this. I'll expect to hear from you." She hung up without my having to say another word or without her even saying good-bye.

These nymphomaniac VonBronigans were getting me down. Oh, I know the masculine version is satyriasis, but somehow with Larry nymphomania seemed the more appropriate word. Up to now I had considered myself open minded. I had always been more than tolerant of the gay movement, and I certainly had been supportive of some of my students who were having problems arising out of their sexual preferences. But Larry was something else, and he was really angering me. It was his kind that made it difficult for guys like me to accept gays on equal terms. Then I told myself that I'd probably asked for it when I wandered into that bar Friday night without looking to see what I was getting into. Live and learn. Well, I hoped I'd have the opportunity to live long enough to use the learning I was acquiring here in Denver. Then this line of thinking brought me back to the BIG problems facing me, and I realized that I must get in touch with Hank.

Having eaten my modest breakfast, I was back in a phone booth dialing the Davis residence. I now had several phone booths that I rotated, real cloak-and-dagger stuff! This time Hank answered.

"Don, how are you? Have you seen the Post this morning? I blush with shame at how we perjured ourselves with the glowing report of the Senator's talk with the rank and file last night, but it seems to me to be the only way we can keep afloat long enough to win the big battle. And do catch tomorrow's issue also; we're going for broke with a favorable report on what we surmise is going on up on Jones Peak."

I replied rather apologetically. "I've not gotten a paper yet, but I will. I thought I saw a man last night that might have been one of your reporters, taking furious notes. Wexler was certainly in full cry, and our speech was a good one, if I do say it myself. It was all lies, of course—promises he has no intention of keeping. I wasn't even sure he knew what he was saying half the time, but I'll give him credit; he does say it very well, more's the pity!"

Then I regaled Hank with a blow by blow description of my Friday night's encounter with Larry and ended by telling him about the phone calls from Larry and Jessamin. As I went over the whole unpleasant encounter with Larry, I realized that all the things he had told me really didn't add much more to what we already knew or what we at least surmised. The one juicy item was the affair between Larry and Bob, but as I had already figured out, that wasn't of much use without something to substantiate the story other than the drunken boasting of one of the participants.

I was a bit miffed at Hank's reaction to this last bit of information. I didn't find the situation at all funny, but he seemed to think it was hilarious.

"Don, you old roué! Who would have thought a sober old professor like you had it in him? First Marilou, then Jessamin, and now the golden boy. And in less than two weeks! You ARE one of the lucky ones. Tell me sometime how you do it. It occurs to me that I'd better keep my eye on my own wife. After all, you might think you have considerable prior claim on her, since you did know her first."

I don't remember what my reply was, but Hank got the message that I definitely was NOT amused. DEFINITELY NOT amused. My God, here I was thinking like Larry and Jessamin again. I'd have to be careful. But the emphasis did seem to get the point across. Hank's amusement had vanished.

"Well, I see your problem, and as I think about it, that does further complicate things. You could go ahead and have a fling with Jessamin and maybe come up with some more dirt, but I doubt that it would have bearing on what we are really after. But I know you wouldn't do that, and going to bed with Platte Valley Pussy, even with double condoms, might be risky. But not as risky as with her brother, so forget that!"

I'm sure I sounded my most professiorial, stuffy self.

"You needn't worry about that! I'm committing perjury with practically every word I say or write these days, but I'll NOT prostitute myself for the cause!" There were those emphasized words again. But I meant it, I REALLY DID!.

Hank was thoughtful.

"By the end of next week, I hope we will have been able to have proof that Wexler flew to Denver the night his wife died. I have had contact with some sources here that indicate they would be willing to instigate an official investigation if I come up with some real proof that would warrant such. Don't turn Larry VonBronigan off too much, because from what you say, he has no real love for his brother-in-law, just carnal love, and he just might be willing to testify against Wexler if he thought it would somehow get Wexler out of the line of inheritance."

I understood Hank's reasoning, but I was appalled!

"Just how the hell am I supposed not to turn off that panting satyr too much? You have no idea what he is like, drunk or sober. He is convinced that I spent part of the night with him; he wants to do it again, he says. If I tell him I'm straight, he'll not believe it. I turn him down, he'll be oh so offended. I can just hear him: 'You dear boy, I am just HEART BROKEN, SIMPLY HEARTBROKEN. I'll kill myself, SIMPLY KILL MYSELF.'"

My imitation of Larry must have been pretty good, too good, in fact. Hank burst into laughter again and then managed to stutter out his rejoinder.

"Oh, I say DEAR BOY, are you SURE you didn't spend the night in Larry's legendary king sized bed?"

I was furious, and in a moment Hank apologized. Then we were back at square one, and he was telling me that he knew I could handle the situation and that something would work out. So again I was told that I was on my own, and Hank Davis couldn't help me. I cursed myself, fate, reunions, Amanda and Marilou, Hank Davis, and most of all, Bob Wexler, and of course, all of the VonBronigans.

Hank was warning me again to be careful—ha!—and not to be alone with Wexler when he came back the next week-end. That was sound advice, but I had a hunch it was easier said than done. I hung up, depressed, scared, and thoroughly out of sorts with life. I slouched back to my duplex, having bought a copy of The Denver Post and a couple of magazines. I tried to read and then to watch television, but all the time I was afraid that the phone would ring. At least I was spared that, and I finally tottered off to bed, trying to get my mind on what Ron and I would be doing during the next week.

CHAPTER 15

Monday and Tuesday were spent in hours of digging through back issues of newspapers, reading more background materials at the library, and lengthy conferences with Ron. There were a couple of meetings with party big-wigs, the first experience I had had with this phase of my job. It was all very exhausting, and I had little time to worry about my VonBronigan problems, or for that matter about solving murderers. It was after a late pick-up dinner Tuesday evening when I got back to the duplex. I'd been home only five minutes when the phone rang. My heart sank, and when I answered, it infact was Larry.

Larry's voice had quite a rational tone about it, and it soon became apparent that the tenor of the conversation was going to be quite different from that of Sunday afternoon.

"Don, I'm glad I found you in. I've called several times, but I know you must be awfully busy. First, I want to apologize for whatever I said Saturday night or Sunday afternoon. I've decided I must have been very out of line. When I drink too much, I don't have good sense. When I called you Sunday, I was still not sober, you know. I'd gotten up feeling awful and started drinking Bloody Marys to taper off, only I didn't really taper off. I just kept on drinking. I do hope I didn't say or do something to offend you. And mostly, I've worried about what happened after you brought me home. I'm usually very careful and use condoms, but of course, I don't remember anything about what we did, so I have to ask you if we took proper protection. I hope you don't mind my asking."

I was delighted by the question. This gave me the opening to say what I'd been wanting to say all along.

"Larry, you needn't worry. Absolutely nothing happened. I took you home, put you to bed, and then left. This gives me the opportunity to say something which probably should have been said before. I'm not gay or bisexual. I wandered into that bar

Saturday night purely by happenstance. I didn't even realize it was a gay bar until you came on to me. I should have said so right then, but you didn't give me much chance to say anything."

Larry sounded honestly appalled.

"You really mean that? What a prick you must think I am! Well, I am, of course, but I hate to have a nice guy like you know it. But don't I remember you fumbling in my crotch in the cab?"

I laughed.

"Well, yes and no. Not in your crotch exactly, though it probably felt like it. I was hunting for your keys so I could get you in your apartment."

There was a moment of silence before Larry replied.

"Oh, my God! What did I tell you about my family and all that? I remember running off the mouth, sort of confessing all sorts of secrets."

"Well, you were a bit indiscreet, but you didn't tell me very much that I didn't already know or hadn't already figured out. Don't worry about it. I'll keep my council."

I was for a moment tempted to follow up with some questions relating to some of the confidences of the Saturday night session, but I decided it wasn't wise to get into that mode again. Larry sounded very relieved.

"Oh, I do trust you. And I'm glad nothing happened. I mean, it's not that I think you might be HIV positive or anything, but when one doesn't know someone very well, or even when one does, one worries. At least when one is sober."

I managed to sound properly stuffy, even censorious. I was sorry. It just came out that way. I was really concerned. When he was sober, Larry could be quite a decent sort of chap.

"Well, I hope you stay sober for a while. You could get yourself into some real trouble if things like Saturday night happen very often."

Larry sighed.

"Yes, I know. Well, I'm sober now, and I'll stay that way tonight at least. There's a meeting at Uncle Karl's, with Dad and

Jessamin. Something to do with a couple of stories in the Denver Post and something about a picture that was taken up at the development on Jones Peak."

This reminded me that I had seen the planted story in the Monday Post, quite as Hank had said it would be. Then I realized what Larry had just said about a picture. I wondered if it were possible that there had been a picture taken of Hank and me. If there had been something like a surveillance camera in the little booth that the watchman came out of, my cover might be blown, as they say. I tried to sound nonchalant, difficult in view of the chills running up my spine.

"What's that about a picture?"

Larry's answer threw no light on the situation.

"I've no idea. Those old farts are up to some of their nasty tricks again, just to make a few more million bucks for their children—and son-in-law—to fight over. I sometimes wish they'd knock it off and become legit. Oh, well, who am I to criticize? Well, I must sign off and get prettied up for the family reunion. Thanks again for not dumping me in the gutter Saturday night—and for not screwing me." And he hung up, with no idea how shaken the bit about a picture had left me.

The charge of adrenaline rushing through me made me forget how tired I was. I went down to a phone booth and called Hank. For a wonder, he was home. His reaction to my report was anything but reassuring.

"Damn! Maybe they saw through the facade of the planted stories in the Post. But the picture business worries me even further. Yes, I think it was very possible that there was a camera in the booth at the gate. There well may have been several pictures showing both sides of the car as we turned around, and front view too. You could easily be identified, in which case, things are really serious. When did you say Wexler was returning to Denver?"

I explained that he had outlined a lot of work to be completed by the time he came back late the next Friday afternoon. There were three appearances over the weekend where he would make talks, one for a large group. There was real urgency in Hank's voice.

"Well, play it as cool as you can, and see if you can find out more about the pictures from Larry. You say you ended up on good terms with him after he called you. But be careful and don't put yourself in any situation with Wexler where he could do you harm. I was hoping you'd call tonight, because late this afternoon I got a call from Joe in Washington with the information that there is indeed a record of Wexler's using his credit card to purchase a ticket from New York to Denver on the fatal night Tillie died. That's strong circumstantial evidence, of course. Whether or not the authorities will consider it enough to open any sort of proceedings against the Senator remains to be seen. He has a lot of clout in a lot of important places, and a lot of money back of him. If he figures out that you might come up with a theory about your friend's death on the snow bank at Jones Peak, backed up by your own experience with the same place, he might just decide that such testimony in addition to what I'm digging up would make you too dangerous to have around, especially since it would be obvious that your presence was all tied in with my attempt to get him."

I was bathed in a cold sweat. I couldn't see any way that I'd get out of this mess with my skin. The conversation was terminated with a few generalities. I went back to the duplex, cursing myself for having allowed myself to get into the mess. I will say for myself, however, that by now I had ceased putting the blame on others. I admitted to myself that I'd been motivated by greed (VonBronigan money), sex (Marilou's presence had muddled my thinking), and some self-righteous, presumptuous notion that I could solve a murder and avenge the death of my friend, Jake Harrell. Stupid, stupid, stupid! I deserved to be knocked off by Bob Wexler, by whatever means he would devise! And then I thought of my family and realized that they didn't deserve to have husband and father murdered by some skunk in Denver. So I resolved to go on, come what might. Did I have any choice...?

Oswald G. Ragatz

I tried to watch television, but the Tuesday evening programs all seemed stupidly shallow or threatening, neither of which helped my frame of mind. I'd just gone into the kitchenette to make myself a sandwich from some bread and cheese I'd picked up at a market the day before, when the phone rang again. I assumed that it would be Jessamin this time, but I doubted that if it were, the outcome of any conversation we might have would be as satisfactory as the conversation with Larry had been. What a delightful surprise it was then when Marilou's voice greeted me!

"I just talked to Amanda, and she tells me that things are really getting dicey! She said that Hank thinks you may be in real danger of bodily harm, as they call it! I'm horrified. I feel partly responsible for your being put in this position."

Two days ago I'd have agreed with her, but now I could honestly say that I was taking full responsibility for being in the spot I was in. From her following remarks, it became obvious that Hank was keeping Amanda up-to-date on all developments, and in turn, Amanda had filled in Marilou pretty thoroughly on what was going on. Marilou even allowed herself a couple of cracks about Jessamin's and Larry's advances. When I rather stiffly responded, she laughed and said that she could understand their interest and she was just glad they hadn't succeeded any better than she had. That just had the effect of causing me embarrassment. Then the conversation took a new direction.

"Don, tomorrow afternoon my friend Bert from New York, the publisher I told you about, will be arriving in Denver. He'll be here 'till after the Fourth of July."

Glad for the new topic of conversation, I interjected what I thought might be a little jibe of my own.

"You mean the guy whose pants you told me to fill."

Marilou was much to slick to have a clumsy remark like that be the last word.

"And they fit you very well. I always fancy a man with a particular build, and you and Bert both fit the bill perfectly. Actually, I want you to meet him, and I am hoping you can have dinner with us tomorrow evening, before we come back up here to my place in the mountains. I'll get to Denver just in time to meet Bert's plane, and I'll have an errand to tend to in East Denver after I pick him up. Then we could pick you up at your apartment about five-thirty. We can have a drink and then go to a nice, quiet restaurant I know so we can have a bit of civilized conversation. After your immersion in Colorado politics and the VonBronigans, I am assuming that you may find the offer attractive."

At first, the offer pleased me inordinately. Then I had an unexpected jab in the solar plexus as Marilou added, "I know you will like Bert. He's really awfully nice."

I couldn't believe it! It had to be jealousy! But why, for God's sake? I had no claim on Marilou, and I'd turned down her offer of an affair with her less than two weeks ago. What a dog in the manger! But that old wound, buried for twenty-six years, all the hurt and jealousy over Marilou's ditching me for Bob Wexler, wasn't completely healed. For a moment, I was infused with the old rage at Bob Wexler, who had stolen Marilou away from me those many years ago, and I then knew I had to see through this project of retribution or die in the attempt. And as Hamlet said, "Ay, there's the rub." During these brief excursions of my brain through these buried emotions, Marilou was telling me how we should meet. I guess that before I'd gone off on my emotional tangent I must have told her that I would like to have dinner with them. Now I had to ask her to repeat what she'd just said.

"I think the connection isn't very good." I was getting quite adept at lying. "Tell me again what you just said."

I don't think I had fooled Marilou one bit, about a bad connection, that is. Whether or not she would figure out why I'd lost concentration, I'll never know. But she was cool as always, cool in the slang sense that is, as she repeated.

"Give me the address of your apartment house, and we'll meet you at the entrance at five-thirty. Just stand outside and watch for us. That way we won't have to find a parking place. I don't know what sort of car I'll be in. That's what I have to do after I pick up Bert. I'm having my car tuned-up by the people who sold it to me, and they'll probably loan me a car for a couple of days. Just watch and you'll see me leaning out of a window expectantly!"

I told her where the building was located and that there was a loading zone directly in front of the entrance where she could park to pick me up. She hung up, leaving me pondering my reactions to the business about Bert. But I realized that I indeed was looking forward to seeing Marilou again, and for sure it would be a change from the company of the VonBronigans, Wexler, and Colorado politics.

Considerably buoyed up by the prospect of dinner with Marilou—even with Bert along—I finished my sandwich, had a glass of milk, listened to the ten-o'clock news, and went to bed. Before I'd gotten to sleep, however, I began to think about Hank's remarks, and I finally had to get up and take a sleeping pill—a rare occurrence. If I were to be creative, cautious, clever, and catch a murderer, I couldn't risk not having enough sleep. The subconscious didn't seem to be affected by the pill, however, so my dreams, though not remembered in detail, were unpleasant and threatening.

CHAPTER 16

I had barely gotten up Wednesday morning when Ron Dawson called me. He had just had a call from Wexler, who had asked us to include a couple of new items in the material we were writing for a talk he was giving on Saturday. He said he'd called Ron so that we could have time to work on it before he got in Friday night. Ron and I were a bit baffled, since the issues at hand were not anything much different from things we had already discussed with him. But we decided that maybe the Senator was just getting a little nervous, though it really wasn't like him.

Then Ron said that Wexler wanted to talk to me and would call me at the duplex about five o'clock. He wanted to be sure that I would be there when he called. I was glad that it wouldn't be any later than that in view of my date with Marilou and her friend Bert. I just hoped that Bob wouldn't talk too long and that he would actually call at five and not much later.

The usual Colorado sunshine had given way to a leaden sky, and occasional rain drops pelted the windows. Fog—or smog—occasionally obscured the taller buildings of the Denver skyline making the general ambience anything but cheery. Even the thoughts of my dinner engagement failed to lift my spirits.

I worked all morning on some material I'd brought home with me, and Ron and I met for a couple of hours in the afternoon at a little office he maintained in an older office building not very far from my apartment. Since it was close, I decided to walk. I should have taken a cab. In spite of my raincoat, my trouser legs were soaked before I got to Ron's office. By the time we had finished our work, the rain had stopped, but there was an icy cold wind blowing down off the mountains. It was nearly five o'clock by the time I got back to the duplex, thoroughly chilled and dispirited.

Oswald G. Ragatz

I hoped that Bob hadn't called me yet. I cleared up some papers that I had spread out on the kitchen table and then went up to the bedroom expecting to take a hot shower before I got dressed for dinner. I was just taking the shirt I'd wear out of a drawer when the doorbell rang. It occurred to me that maybe Marilou's visit to her garage hadn't taken as long as she had expected and that they had parked and decided to come on up to the apartment. I'd not told her my number or floor, but then there was a doorman, manager really, who could have told her where I lived. So it was with pleasant expectation that I dashed down the stairs and opened the door.

It was with considerable shock and then dismay that I saw Senator Robert Wexler standing there. He didn't wait for me to ask him in—which I suppose I might have done out of habit—but shoved past me, taking the door from my hand and closing it firmly behind us. He had a look on his face that was quite indescribable, a combination of anger, hostility, and yet also possibly fright. I wouldn't begin to guess what my expressive features displayed. I wasn't dissembling, that was for sure!

"Good old reliable Don," he snarled. "I asked you to be here at five o'clock and here you are. I knew I could depend on you. One always can depend on a friend, can't one?"

But his words were dripping pure acid. I was petrified.

My mind was racing at top speed, surprisingly clear in spite of the peril I was sure I was facing. Bob was supposed to be in Washington until Friday. He had made sure that Ron Dawson knew that he wouldn't be returning to Denver until Friday afternoon, but he had also made sure that I would be in my duplex at five o'clock today. There was no doubt in my mind that he had made a secret trip to Denver on a late afternoon flight once before for the sole purpose of murder. It seemed pretty obvious that he had decided that what had worked once would work again.

But I couldn't ponder all this any more at the moment. Bob was talking, and I had to listen.

"There are a few things that need to be cleared up, my old friend. But before getting down to details, I want to say that I always resented your superior attitude to me. You were always so damn smart, and you always thought that Bob Wexler just wasn't in your league. Well, you were wrong. I out-smarted you at every turn. All those times you thought you were helping me out with term papers and exams I was laughing behind your back at the sucker that you were. I had a lot of extra leisure time I'd not have had if I'd had to study myself. And you've done it again, getting all this stuff together for my campaign. It's been very useful. You could have made a nice little bundle of cash and then gone back to your second-rate campus in Jeffreysville, none the wiser to the fact that I'd paid you half of what a real professional would have cost."

I had been shaking from fright and now from anger, but I hated to have Bob see how distraught I really was. I thought I'd be more able to cope if we weren't standing up, so I indicated that maybe we should sit down and talk about whatever was bothering him, not that I didn't know. I had the impression that Bob also was glad not to be standing, but he continued his tirade as we sat down.

"But you couldn't let well enough alone, you great brain. You had to cozy up to that bastard Hank Davis and start making trouble. I don't know which of you thought up the bright idea of tracking down the fact that I flew out to Denver from New York the night my second wife killed herself, but I have a hunch it was none other than you, old smart-ass Donald Moffett. And don't try to deny that there's been a lot of snooping going on in Washington. I've been in the nation's capitol long enough to have some pretty good contacts myself, and I can match Hank Davis and his goddamn buddies play for play."

Bob was shaking with rage by now, hardly able to control his voice. He had to stop to get his breath, which gave me a chance to speak. I doubt that I was in control of my voice any more than he was, but self-preservation made it imperative that I try to defuse the situation.

"Bob, I had no idea you felt that way about me. I'm sorry if anything I did made you hate me so. And it is a cinch I have no contacts in Washington that might be making any problems for you now. Why would...."

That was as far as I got before he interrupted me.

"Did! Did, you bastard! Are doing! I don't know why you decided to stab me in the back, but I know what you and Hank are up to. Uncle Karl called me last night with the very interesting information that there were pictures taken at the gate to the development on Jones Peak, and who should be sitting in the car with Hank Davis but Donald Moffett! The license plate had already verified the fact that it was Davis's car. My father-in-law and Karl are furious with me for putting you on my payroll. They were fooled for twenty-four hours by the article in the Monday Post, but now we all see it as a plant to throw us off the scent. You were hired to be on my side, but now it is obvious you are working for the opposition. I can't see that you have anything political to gain by the dirty trick, so it has to be personal. You're just getting back at me for taking your girl away from you twenty-six years ago, and that bitch Amanda has probably fed you a lot of crap about how I walked out on her and her stupid dad's law firm. It's obvious that you told Davis about our development on Jones Peak, and since you knew how to get there, you took him there, you son-of-a-bitch!"

Of course, I hadn't remembered how to get there, but I had indeed filled in Hank with a number of details about previous activities on Jones Peak. It was now obvious that Bob hadn't forgotten the episode of our camp-out on Jones Peak years ago! This further convinced me that our theories had been valid. Not that that was going to do anyone much good if he got me, a prime witness as it were, out of the way. I was sure that he was here for just that purpose. It only remained to be seen just when or how. He had taken the chair nearest to the door, and he was taller and in better condition than I was, though not nearly as heavy, so my making a bolt for the door seemed quite hopeless.

He glared at me for a bit, and then he seemed to have read my mind.

"So, my fine friend," he growled, "you have memories of a glacier on Jones Peak. Well, why don't we just renew that old experience and take a little ride up there right now? You wanted to know what was going on at our old camping spot, so now you can see it first hand. I'm catching the red eye back to New York at eleven, so there's plenty of time for a little visit. We can chat on the way up. Of course, I assume you know all about flight schedules from New York to Denver and back." His voice dripped sarcasm with this last remark.

I inferred from these comments that he had found out about the investigations that Joe what-ever-his-name-was had been making into Bob's activities on the night Tillie died. Once again, someone I had counted on had proven to be less than reliable. Bob stood up, but I remained in my chair, trying to look calm as I replied to his suggestion of a trip to the mountains.

"I can't possibly go tonight. I have a dinner engagement a little later on. I was just getting ready to..."

But Bob interrupted, his voice forged steel.

"That is one dinner engagement that will not be kept. You are still in my employ, and if I want us to take a ride, we'll take a ride!"

I thought of telling him that I was to be picked up shortly by Marilou and that if I weren't here, a search would be made for me. But the look on Bob's face indicated that there would be no reasoning with him. Anyway, something told me that it would not be a good idea to bring Marilou into the conversation. Bob was beyond any rational thinking. How far beyond became immediately apparent. He still had on his raincoat, and I now realized that he had kept his hand in the right pocket through all this, even though he was sitting down. Now as he stood up, he removed his hand, which held a pistol. I know absolutely nothing about guns, but I knew this one was for real. I figured that if I refused to go with him or put up a struggle, I'd be shot then and there. My only hope seemed to be in gaining time, for

Oswald G. Ragatz

what I couldn't imagine, but maybe when we got down to the street, I could somehow get away from him. I was instantly out of my chair and in a moment was being pushed to the door.

Bob opened the door and looked out into the foyer, which was empty. There were only two other units on this floor, and I don't think either of them were presently occupied. He put the hand with the gun back in his pocket, but it was obvious that I was covered. We got into the elevator, but instead of punching the ground level button, Bob pushed the garage button. So much for my idea of escaping when we got to the street. It was obvious now how he had come in. Of course, as a family member he might have access to the key-card which permitted residents of the building to enter the garage whenever they wished. I prayed that the elevator would stop at some other floor for another passenger, but no such luck. Bob kept his finger on the down button. Whether that would prevent a stop or not I had no idea.

We reached the garage, and Bob snarled, "I've got the gun on you. Don't try to break away, or they'll find the victim of a hold-up spattered all over the damn garage."

A big SUV was parked illegally near the elevator door. Since it was not any car I'd seen Bob drive before, it was pretty obvious that he had rented it at the airport so as not to have his own car seen. He yanked open the door on the driver's side and gave the order.

"Get in this side and slide across. In case you have any idea of jumping out of the other side, forget it! I've jammed the door so it can't be opened. Then he sneered, "And I've activated the 'child protection' window locks. Now I'm a good one-handed driver, and if you try any funny stuff with me, I'll pull this trigger. Mess with my driving and I'll crash us. We might both be killed, but at this point I've nothing to loose if you and your big mouth are still around. So what the hell."

He threw the car into reverse, then forward to the exit door, which he quickly activated by putting the key card in the slot in the mechanism mounted on a nearby post on the driver's side of

Reunion With Murder

the car. I didn't think there was anyone in the garage, but if there had been, there would have been nothing to arouse suspicion. I had obeyed Bob's orders, and with that gun in Bob's hand pointed in my general direction, though back inside his pocket, I was not tempted to engage in any creative counter maneuvers.

We sped out of the garage and made two left-turns, which brought us onto the one-way street in front of the building. We swung into traffic behind a Lincoln Continental that had its left turn signals on. The driver obviously was planning to swing to the left into the loading zone in front of the building's entrance so that he could park there. But Bob was in a hurry, and with a blast of his horn he swung to the left of the Continental, through the no-parking zone, and drove back into traffic in front of the Continental. As I heard the squeal of tires to my right when the driver of the Continental jammed on the brakes, I got just a glimpse into the big car. There were people in both front and back seats, and for an instant I thought of Hank Davis, but that seemed totally improbable. I put it down to a bit of mad, wishful thinking on my part and the fact that Amanda drove a Continental. I pushed the idea out of my thoughts as we wove our way through rush-hour traffic. I kept hoping that we'd be stopped by the police for speeding, but no such luck. Before long we were on I-25, and then a few minutes later we switched to I-70 toward the mountains. It wasn't till we were well into the foot-hills before anything was said. I decided to make a try at reasoning with Bob. One shouldn't just meekly submit to being murdered without putting forth some sort of effort.

"Bob, don't foul up your life by doing something stupid because you are angry with me. I don't know what you are planning to do with me or why we're going to Jones Peak, but whatever it is, you'll eventually be found out, and that'll be the end of your career. Anyway, you'll not be able to live with yourself if you'd killed an old friend."

The minute I said this, I knew how fatuous it was. Senator Wexler had lived for quite some time with two murders on his conscience, a friend and a wife. And I was implying that he had a conscience, which I doubted. To outward appearances he had lived very well. One more murder would hardly bother him. I was not surprised at his sarcastic reply, delivered as we sped past three trucks on an up grade on a curve.

"Well, now, just listen to our goodie, goodie little preacher man! I learned early in life that there is just one person that matters in the world, and that's Bob Wexler. If Bob Wexler wants something or someone, he gets it, one way or another. And no nonsense about what you other fools call conscience. Oh, I had to learn to be efficient. I blew my first try at getting you out of the way so that I could have a go at your girlfriend and a chance for a job with her dad. But that was a good lesson, and I never made that mistake a second time, you can be sure!"

The cards were all out on the table, as it were, so I allowed myself a cryptic remark.

"Yes, as poor Jake found out." And then I added, "I wonder if he realized you'd planned to have him killed, just as he was unable to stop himself from going over the edge at the end of the glacier."

I was appalled at Bob's reply.

"Well, I certainly hope so. He was so goddamn smug about his beloved Amanda. Both you and he thought old Bobbie Wexler couldn't get a woman for himself. Well, I got both your women, and they WERE charming bed companions for a while, AND I might add, they helped my career as well. Which brings us up to the present and prompts me to point out that if you think all this effort I went to to get where I am is going to be wasted because of your meddlings, you've got another think coming!"

Discouraged by my brief attempt at conversation, I sat in rigid silence. I began to wonder if Bob would even have a chance to use the gun. His anger was prompting him to drive much too fast for the wet roads, and with just the left hand at that. I was sure we would crash on one of the curves, but the heavy car held the road in spite of the driver's recklessness. As we got higher into the mountains, I could see a slight dusting of white on the trees. It was unusual for snow at this time of year, but not unheard of. There had been a reason for that frigid wind blowing down into Denver during the afternoon.

It seemed that we had driven hours in grim silence before Bob turned off onto the side road, and then after a bit into the lane that led up to the VonBronigan development on Jones Peak. By now there was enough snow to pretty well cover the ground. There was still a little light, though the low clouds and precipitation had made it necessary to turn on the headlights. In order to do this, Bob had taken his left hand off the steering wheel, which he then held firmly with his left knee while he flipped on the lights. His right hand had remained in his coat pocket, holding the gun throughout the trip. This made the whole driving process even more frightening, of course.

We came to a skidding halt at the gate, the headlights catching the watchman as he emerged from his little booth. He came around to the driver's side and flashed his flashlight into the car. I could see that it was the same big goon that had turned Hank and me back a few days before. His voice showed considerable surprise.

"Oh, hello Senator. I certainly didn't expect to see you up here, not at this time of day anyway."

Bob was all affability.

"It's good to see you again, Hernando. By the way, do you recognize my friend here?"

Hernando turned his light in my face. He sounded baffled and a little worried when he answered.

"Why yes, I think I do. He looks like the same guy that was in that car I chased out a week or so ago, the one the bosses wanted pictures of. Did I do something wrong? They didn't have a pass or anything, so I followed orders and told them to get out."

Bob continued his friendly act, his voice reassuring and smooth.

"No problem, Hernando. There was just a little misunderstanding. Professor Moffett here is helping me with my campaign. He wants to see some of the development up here, so I decided I'd run him up since he didn't get to see it the last time he was here. Just open the gate for us, and we'll drive on up to the big shed."

For a moment, I had thought of trying to get help from Hernando, but then I knew that would be useless. Bob's coat pocket was bulging in the direction of my stomach, and there was little doubt in my mind where Hernando's loyalty lay.

Hernando shrugged.

"Well, O.K. Senator. But it's pretty slippery up there. They worked about two hours this morning, just getting the loaded trucks backed up to the drop off at the bottom of the ski slope. But it got too cold and wet, so everyone knocked off work for the rest of the day. They just left the trucks up there ready to start dumping when they get back to work, hopefully in the morning. You'll have to watch it if you walk around any. It's freezing a little, I think, and the snow will make things pretty slippery. Anyway, it's muddy. Do you want me to go with you?"

Bob's reply was very quick.

"Oh, no, Hernando. You stay here at the gate. You never can tell when you'd be needed here."

Hernando shrugged, and said something to the effect that he doubted that there would be anyone snooping around in this weather at this time of day. But he unlocked the big gate, and then he handed the flashlight in to Bob as we drove on into the compound.

CHAPTER 17

We drove for a quarter of a mile on a rough road that was thinly black-topped. Heavy machinery parked by the side of the road could be seen dimly. Then after a bend in the road, the silhouettes of the partly finished condos loomed up, stretching up the mountain-side. For a moment there was a break in the clouds, and in the twilight I saw the scaffolding of the ski jump. The dusting of snow made it fairly easy to see things as long as there was any light at all. Then Bob turned the car toward the down-slope, and in a moment he had parked by a long building, presumably what was called the shed. There was a bright outside light extending above a high door, which undoubtedly opened to admit trucks or other heavy machinery. Bob took the gun out of his pocket, and getting out of the car, he indicated that I should slide across and get out too.

Nothing had been said up to this point, other than occasional cursings about Hank Davis or me. Now Bob seemed to want to talk. Actually, part of the time he seemed to be talking to himself more than to me as we felt our way along crushed gravel paths and occasionally on planks that had been put over particularly muddy places. He seemed to be in no hurry to get on with the matter at hand, namely killing me, which was all right with me! At times it almost seemed as though he might be giving me a friendly tour of the development.

"The outdoor pool is over there behind that first group of condos. They are the smaller, three-room units, six units on three floor in each building. Those larger ones farther up the hill have two bedrooms. They all have balconies, as you can see. Then at the top up there are twelve buildings with the luxury units, two to a building. They have three bedrooms, three baths, and will have all the luxury items you can imagine. There is area to add more units later on. The ski lift starts up there by the big jobs. There's a parking area up there for the drive-ins. You can't see the lift from here, though it's finished. It goes up beyond the trees, along side of the glacier. There will be snow machines for those times when the snow melts too much, though up here there won't be much need for that, with the ice underlay."

Bob gave me a nudge with the gun, indicating that I should turn toward the down slope. Then his mind seemed to be preoccupied. As we stumbled on a few yards, he was talking to himself.

"I wonder if I can trust that bastard, Hernando. But of course, he won't question an accident. He said to watch out 'cause it was slippery."

Then Bob's attention seemed to turn to me again.

"I say, ol' buddy, this looks different from the last time we were up here, doesn't it?"

I didn't know whether he expected me to answer or not, but I had to do something to break the tension. My voice sounded very strange to me.

"Did you really intend for me to go over the edge when I slid down the snow on that disc?"

Bob grunted.

"Well, now, what do you think? I expect I really did. It seemed an easy way to get rid of the competition. Of course, I needn't have worried. It was easy to get Marilou away from you without going to the trouble of bumping you off. You were such a wimp! She was ready for some action. She told me you'd never even tried to lay her. Incredible!"

He was determined to taunt me, and I had no response. It would just be futile and would give him more satisfaction. By now we had come up to the place where the first of several big trucks, loaded with dirt and rubble, were lined up, presumably ready to dump their loads over the edge of the drop-off when the weather cleared. Bob started to talk again, in mock, tour-guide manner.

"Now just ahead of us we have an historic spot. If rocks could talk, they would tell some interesting tales. Does anyone in the group have a question? Oh, you, the little man up ahead of me, you want to know if this is the same spot you saw once long ago. Well, yes it is. The drop-off is to be filled so that the slope from the ski jump will level off down into the meadow below. There's a lot of dirt going to be dumped in there, probably tomorrow, and it will bury any unpleasant debris that might be down there wedged in the rocks below. I doubt that anyone would notice."

Then his mind seemed to wander again, and he was half talking to himself.

"Now I hadn't thought about Hernando. If he notices that there is only one person leaving, I'll have to tell him that there was an accident, but then people would find out that I'd been here. Very messy. Damn. I'd figured Hernando wouldn't be here so late."

Bob was having doubts, as well he might. He may have thought he was smart, but he surely hadn't thought this operation through very carefully. I thought I'd try to work on his uncertainty. We were standing by the last of the trucks now. Some sixteen-foot long boards had been put along the edge of the drop off where the original slope had been cut down a bit so there wouldn't need to be as much fill after the drop-off. I suppose the boards had been put there to make it easier for the truck drivers to negotiate the mud when they got out of their vehicles. This made the ski slope along here even steeper than it had originally been. I was standing probably only four feet from the end of the board and from the drop-off to the rocks below.

"Bob, this isn't going to work. Don't you think there are going to be questions asked when I just disappear, presuming that I'm buried beneath all this dirt? And if Hernando sees you leaving alone he'll...."

Bob interrupted angrily.

"You and your fucking logic again. You think you are so damn smart! Do you think I'd hesitate to put a bullet through Hernando? Hardly, after killing Jake, and Tillie, and you!"

This was the first mention of Tillie. There was a moment of silence, while Bob's brain was trying to sort out the situation. Then he brightened up.

"Oh, neat! You'll be found with the gun. Obviously you shot Hernando but slipped and fell to your untimely death. I'll tell the authorities that Hank Davis and you probably came up here. We have the pictures of your first visit. That will take care of that son-of-a-bitch, too. He'll be an accessory after the fact."

In spite of myself, I felt that I was getting into a sort of intriguing debate. I had been very good at that sort of thing back in college when I was on the debate team. Now the stakes were high—my life! This made for maximum motivation! I had no other choice.

"But why would Hank come up here and kill the watchman?"

"I didn't say Hank killed the watchman!" Bob screamed. "I said YOU killed him. The gun will be with YOU!"

"But why would Hank want ME to kill the watchman?"

"You shit-head! Because he wanted to know what was going on up here so he could get those environmentalists on our backs. The watchman tried to stop you and you shot him."

"And then Hank drives your rented car back to the airport, a car with a jammed door, charged to your credit card, probably?" I took a chance on that one.

But this last argument was too much for Senator Wexler. He screamed with rage and frustration.

"I don't know what the hell I'm going to do, but I'll figure something out without the help of your goddamn brain. Now shut up and get going. Either I shoot you in the head right here or you go over the edge like you were supposed to twenty-six years ago."

During these last tense moments, my brain had been working on two levels. One level was arguing with Bob, the other was making note of a fact that might save my life. I had stepped back toward the far end of the plank on which we were standing. The ground was uneven, and I had realized that my end of the board was probably as much as a foot off the ground. I now was two or three feet from my end, but Bob was on the far end, a bit above me. We were on a sort of teeter totter, actually. I'd been facing Bob during my attempt to talk my way out of the predicament. Now I turned my back to Bob as though I'd decided on the option of jumping off the edge rather than being shot. But I jumped up as high as I could and only a little forward, landing on the end of the plank with as much force as I could muster. Thanks to that extra weight around my middle, there was enough leverage that Bob was thrown off balance. Actually, I think that he probably went up in the air a little and then stumbled to the side where the earth had been graded away. He slid down onto the wet ski slope, now even slicker because of the light coating of snow. I would have gone over the edge onto the rocks below myself had I not been able to catch myself on the back of the truck that was waiting to dump the first load of the fill. I hadn't had time to look back to see what had happened to Bob, but my ears told me all I needed to know. There was a terrified scream, a wild shot as his finger automatically tightened on the trigger, then a partial sentence that trailed off into nothing: "You fuckin' basta..." There was a faint thump from somewhere below and then silence.

Or maybe I didn't hear a thump. I'll never know. My heart was thumping, that was for sure. I clung on to some sort of rod that went up the back corner of the truck, probably part of the dumping mechanism. I must have stood there clutching the rod at least five minutes, my hand nearly frozen stiff, half expecting to see Bob emerge over the edge, gun in hand. Or maybe his ghost?

Finally I became aware that there was a light snow falling, and that I had no coat on. I was just in my shirt-sleeves, and I was very cold. My shivering wasn't just from fright. I suppose the chill brought me to my senses, and I began to do some thinking about my own problem. I realized that I would have to cope with Hernando first. I didn't know whether or not Bob had left the keys in the car. If he hadn't, they were in his pocket, in the mess that undoubtedly existed on the rocks below. I wasn't about to try to get down there to find keys! For some outrageous reason, I was momentarily reminded of my hunting for keys in Larry's pockets while we rode in the taxi.

I began to inch my way back on the boards, now very conscious how unstable and slippery they were. I'd just gotten to the crushed-rock path that had ended shortly before the last of the parked trucks when I became aware of the sounds of cars, and I thought I heard a siren in the direction of the gate. By the time I'd gotten to the shed and the parked SUV, headlights were approaching along the bumpy, black-topped lane—three sets of them. I didn't know whether to be relieved or scared. But I figured that nothing could be as bad as had been my predicament ten minutes before. Then I realized that the lead car was obviously an official vehicle, since it had a revolving red light on its top. The second car pulled up along side just as the headlights of the sheriff's car caught me in full view. I saw the elegant front of a Lincoln Continental. Two officers jumped out of the first vehicle, and only seconds later, four people piled out of the Continental—first Hank Davis, then a man I didn't know but who was about my size and shape, and then Marilou and Amanda. By now the other officer's car had pulled up, and two more officers and the watchman emerged.

Now if I had had the opportunity to choreograph this scene the way I would have wanted it to be, I would have dramatically described my abduction and my clever dispatch of Senator Wexler. Then I would have been roundly congratulated for my bravery and ingenuity. But, alas, I had only a couple of seconds to wonder how all these people had known about something that had happened only ten minutes ago. Then I passed out—out cold on the snowy, wet ground before anyone could catch me. That was just what I needed—more cold, wet clothes.

The next episode couldn't have been improved upon, however. When I finally regained consciousness, lying on some sort of table in the storage shed, two lovely ladies were fussing over me, actually taking off some of my clothes. As reason returned, I realized that they were just getting the wet shirt off my cold back so someone could put a blanket around me. Of course, I'd have chickened out if it had been anything else but that. This was no James Bond novel, for all of its bizarre aspects, and I was no James Bond, that was for sure.

It took quite some time before the question and answer period was over. I think someone asked me what had happened, and though my teeth were still chattering, after a few feeble starts I got my wits together enough to give a fairly lucid report of the events from the time I answered the door of my duplex to the moment I heard Senator Wexler's curse die away as he went over the edge. Throughout all this, I was aware of that big lug, Hernando, standing to one side, watching with scared eyes, and when I got to the part where Bob had said he would have to shoot Hernando, I thought there might be another fainting patient.

Two of the officers, flashlights in hand, departed to try to negotiate the drop-off and find Bob's body. Now it was my turn to ask questions. Marilou, the Davises, and Bert—he was introduced to me somewhere during all this—all of them sort of talked at once. I could not attempt to give a specific report of the dialogue. However, it went something like this, and an improbable story it was. But thank God, it was true.

Marilou had decided to include Amanda and Hank in our dinner with Bert. She had come to Denver earlier than she had planned and had dropped her car off at the garage before going to the airport. Hank and Amanda had picked her up at the garage. They were a little early getting to the airport, so they had parked the Continental and went in to wait for Bert at the luggage pick up. Much to their surprise, just after Bert had claimed his luggage, they saw Senator Wexler coming from the Avis car-rental desk, key in hand. They ducked around a corner so that they would not be seen, but Wexler's appearance at the airport aroused their suspicions. It smacked of what we had surmised had happened once before—a mid-week trip to Denver from New York, by a man who was supposed to be in Washington.

Hank then tried to call me at the duplex, but of course I'd not gotten there yet. It took them a little while to get the Continental from where they had parked it, and the traffic was heavy getting into the city, so they had decided the best thing was to get to me as soon as they could. Actually, they were driving up to the front of my building when Wexler cut in to pass them on the left. I had indeed correctly recognized the Davis Continental, and most fortunately both Hank and Marilou, who was sitting in back on the left side of the car, recognized me as we sped by. I must have had my face pasted on the window in fright. They immediately figured out that I was being abducted, though they had no idea where Bob was taking me. Fortunately, there was a cell phone in Amanda's car. They immediately alerted police and the sheriff and then took off following Wexler and me. It was a wild ride in heavy traffic, and by the time they got to the foot-hills, they had lost sight of the SUV. A sheriff had joined their dash somewhere past Golden, and another joined in the chase shortly thereafter. Thanks to the phone, Hank could keep in touch with the officers.

It was Marilou and Amanda that had first opined that Wexler was heading for Jones Peak, and the more they talked about it, the more they figured that was a good guess. Hank remembered how to get to Jones Peak so was able to lead the officers' cars up the little road to the gate at the development. The presence of the law had easily convinced Hernando to let them through, and that's how they found me.

There would be grim activity at the Jones Peak development throughout much of the night, but the Davis car soon was bearing its original passengers and a bedraggled and thoroughly exhausted political science professor back to civilization. It was during the ride down from the mountains that the reality of what had just transpired began to sink in. I began to realize that I had actually been responsible for the death of another human being, not a comfortable feeling at all. I finally said something to my friends about my feelings. They all tied into me at once. If I hadn't done what I did, I'd be the one lying at the bottom of the drop-off. The man I had flipped over the edge was a killer and a thoroughly immoral and amoral individual. The possibility of our having been able to prove that he had murdered before was problematic, but now retribution had eliminated our need to pursue our project any further. And on and on. I had to agree with all that they said, but I will never quite be able to forget the terrified scream and the half completed curse I heard as Bob went over the edge. He had once upon a time been my friend—at least, I had thought so.

We went back to the duplex where I first took a long, hot shower and then got into dry clothes. In the meantime, my "guests" ordered out for pizza, not the chic dinner Marilou had planned for us, but it was certainly appreciated by all.

We were just finishing the last of the food when the first batch of police arrived. I don't know what luck I would have had convincing people of my bizarre tale if Hank Davis had not been there. Of course, there had been ample reports from the sheriffs that had been on the scene. Hernando was being questioned as a witness, and he was turning out to be an ace up our sleeve. When the flashlight had been handed to Bob, Hernando had noticed that Wexler had been driving with one hand, his right hand in a bulging coat pocket. I don't know how really bright Hernando was, but he was street-wise. He had already put two and two together before he heard the wild shot fired as Bob fell onto the slope. Since Hernando had recognized me as having been the same man who had been in the car with Hank Davis, he figured something wasn't right.

After more questioning by the police, my friends insisted I go to bed. Hank had called someone to be sure that the Post would have the scoop in the death of Colorado's incumbent Senator. It was assumed that the VonBronigans had been notified, and Jessamin, of course. Thank God, I was spared that trauma.

Oswald G. Ragatz

I slept like I hadn't slept for weeks. It was mid-morning when I awoke to the smell of coffee, frying bacon, and toast coming from down-stairs. I looked in the mirror and realized that whoever it was preparing breakfast shouldn't be subjected to the haggard face peering back at me. I took a shower, shaved, and put on casual clothes.

When I got downstairs, Marilou and Bert were sitting at the table reading the morning Post. There was a rumpled bed visible in the guest room off the foyer. Under less unusual circumstances, I probably would have experienced one of those silly jabs of jealousy in my gut, but as it was, I just felt eternally grateful for having such loyal friends.

I could see the banner headlines on the front page of The Denver Post they were reading. SENATOR WEXLER FALLS TO DEATH DURING KIDNAP ATTEMPT. Hank must have had them stop the presses, considering how late it must have been when he called in the story. I realized that I had had little sense of time once I had answered that fatal ring of my doorbell at five o'clock the evening before. I just remembered that it was totally dark by the time we had started down from the mountain through intermittent snow showers.

After a relaxed breakfast, I decided that I should call Lucille. Somehow it didn't occur to me that she would be totally unaware of the events of the past twenty-four hours. She was just leaving to teach her first class when I called.

I blurted out, "I just wanted you to know that I'm alright."

Her bemused answer brought things into perspective.

"That's nice. And so am I. But I miss you. I'll be glad when this summer job of yours is over and you come home."

I realized that there was no time to go into all the sordid details of my "summer job." I told her that my job would be finished much sooner than I'd expected and that I hoped to be back in Jeffreysville in a few days.

"Oh, that will be wonderful, Don. I'll be waiting for you with open arms. Now I must run, but call me tonight and tell me what it's all about."

So my class reunion had come full circle. Of course, there were several days before I could take that plane back to the Midwest. There were more question sessions, during which the information revealed by Wexler's own words, supported by our various surmises, brought out into the open many of the sordid details of Senator Wexler's rise to power. It became public knowledge that the Senator had probably murdered his wife Tillie, and Hank saw to it that there was mention of the strong possibility that Wexler had also murdered his friend, Jake Harrell, twenty-four years earlier.

At no time did I have to communicate with the senior VonBronigans. They assumed a remarkably low profile through the whole mess, though the Denver Post did print a number of insinuations as to dirty work on Jones Peak as far as the condo development was concerned. Since the episode of Wexler's death occurred at the site of "Little Aspen on the Eastern Slope," there was no way that could be kept secret any longer. There were bound to be major investigations into that operation.

The grieving widow Jessamin was conspicuous for her absence in the press. Whether or not she mourned the loss of her prominent husband, I'll never know. My own guess was that it was just all very inconvenient. I had gotten the impression in my various contacts with her that she perhaps had been feeling that the Senator thing was getting a bit out of hand. Larry's remarks also had indicated as much.

I had my bags packed, had turned in the keys to the duplex to the manager, and was waiting for Hank to take me to the airport. My rented car, paid for by the VonBronigans, had been picked up a couple of days earlier by a taciturn minion sent by "The Group." At least they hadn't evicted me from my abode. The doorbell rang at the same time the phone rang. I quickly let Hank in and then answered the phone. To my amazement, it was Larry.

"I'm SO glad I got you before you left. I just want to tell you that I appreciate what you have DONE for my sister and me. We both KNEW what Wexler was up to, you know, wanting to get his filthy hands on our inheritance. We had figured out that he had undoubtedly killed Tillie, and Jessamin was SCARED to death that the same thing could happen to her. She knew she was safe as long as the two old men were alive, but once they were dead, it would just have been a matter of time. Of course, I'd probably have been out of the way by then, one way or another. I don't know how you did it, but thanks for BOTH of us. Jessamin would have called, but she is off to The Cote d'Azure with her latest lover. She was sort of mad at you anyway, I think, because she couldn't get to first base with you. She's not used to being rejected. I'm not either, for that matter, but it's sort of interesting to be—rejected, that is. It gives one that common touch somehow, something lacking in us VonBronigans. Well, ta, ta, dear boy. Go back to your college and tell the little dears how it REALLY is out in the jungle."

Other than "hello," I'd not said a word. Nor was there anything TO say. I was glad Larry had called, though. It took care of some loose ends. I turned to Hank and said, "Let's get to the airport. I don't want to disappoint those loving arms waiting for me back home. I just HATE to keep anyone waiting!"

ABOUT THE AUTHOR

Oswald G. Ragatz, Professor Emeritus of Organ at Indiana University's renowned School of Music, has degrees from the University of Denver, the Eastman School of Music, and the University of Southern California, with further study at Juilliard School of Music and Union Theological Seminary School of Sacred Music. After his retirement from his post as Chairman of the Organ Department at Indiana University and an extensive career as concert organist throughout the United States and Europe, he decided to begin a new career as a writer of mystery novels. Two books have so far resulted, Reunion with Murder and Murder Makes a Man (in preparation). He hopes that the plots will be sufficiently original to compensate for any lack of colorful writing. He found it difficult to get away from a pedantic style of expression, the result of more than four decades of supervising dissertations and the writing of his own textbook, Organ Technique: A Basic Course of Study (published by The Indiana University Press and re-published by TIS music publishers).